Texas Daze

WHISPERING SPRINGS, TEXAS
BOOK NINE

CYNTHIA D'ALBA

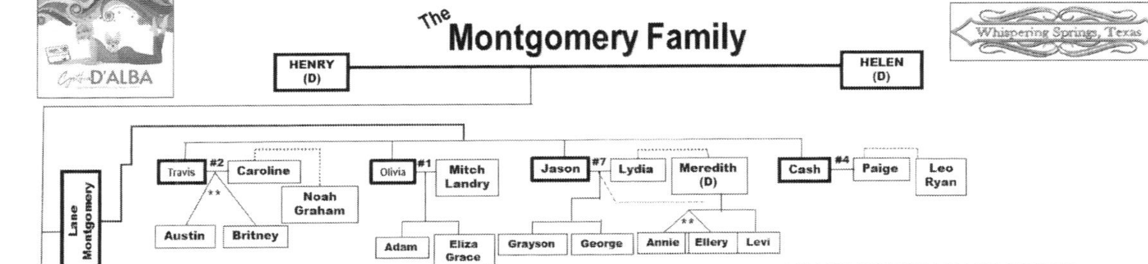
D'ALBA
The Montgomery Family
HENRY (D)
HELEN (D)
Lane Montgomery
Travis
#2
Caroline
Noah Graham
Austin
Britney
**
Olivia
#1
Mitch Landry
Adam
Eliza Grace
Jason
#7
Lydia
Meredith (D)
Grayson
George
Annie
Ellery
Levi
**
Cash
#4
Paige
Leo Ryan
Clint Montgomery
KC
#3
Drake Gentry
Reno
#5
Magda
Darren
#6
Porchia
**
Cora Montgomery Singer-Cooper
Marc Singer
#11
Jennifer
Chloe
Dax Cooper
#10
Cori
Samantha Cooper
1. Texas Two Step (M)
2. Texas Tango (M)
3. Texas Fandango (M)
4. Texas Twist (M)
5. Texas Bossa Nova (M)
6. Texas Hustle (M)
7. Texas Lullaby (M)
8. Saddles & Soot (F)
9. Texas Daze (F)
#10 A Texan's Touch (M)
#11 Texas Bombshell (M)

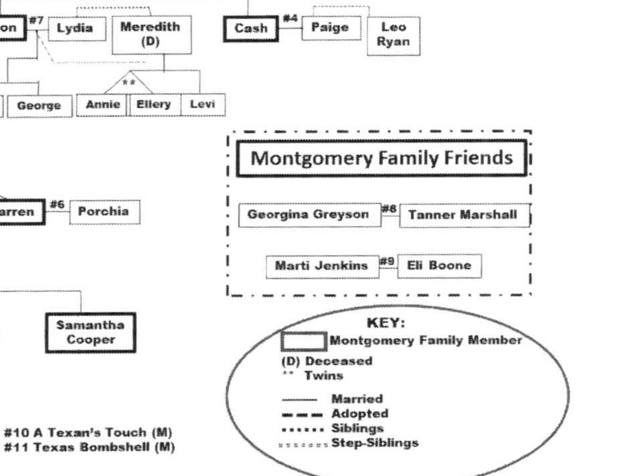
Whispering Springs, Texas
Montgomery Family Friends
Georgina Greyson
#8
Tanner Marshall
Marti Jenkins
#9
Eli Boone
KEY:
Montgomery Family Member
(D) Deceased
** Twins
Married
Adopted
Siblings
Step-Siblings

To my readers.
Without you, I couldn't do what I love.
THANK YOU.

To Martha Gale Caseman Henderson
Hope you enjoy your namesake's story!

Copyright

Texas Daze

Print ISBN: 978-1-9468990-6-4

Digital ISBN: 978-0-9982650-9-4

Cover Artist: Elle James

Editor: Kelli Collins

One

"Goddamn gophers." Martha Gale Jenkins adjusted the tree limb she'd found to use as a crutch. She limped alongside her horse as they made their way back to the barn, her ankle hot and throbbing. "Hate 'em, hate 'em, hate 'em."

Rascal, her chestnut gelding, limped along with her. Both of them had fallen victim to a couple of new gopher holes in the lower pasture. Better she fall in than Rascal. Hell, he was probably more valuable to the ranch than she was.

She was still a ways out when Pedro, one of the young ranch hands, came riding toward them.

"Seen ya limpin', Marti. Need some help?"

Martha, aka Marti, was in a right fine mood, ready to pick a fight with anybody just to take her mind off the pain in her left leg. But Pedro was too nice a guy for her to use as her personal punching bag. "Thanks, Pedro. Rascal and me had a run-in with a couple of rattlesnakes followed up by new gopher holes." She pointed to two lifeless rattlesnakes draped over her saddle. "Won one battle, lost the other."

The eighteen-year-old shook his head. "Can't believe you brought those snakes home wit cha."

"You've been here long enough to know that Grisham loves rattlesnake meat. It'll put him in a good mood for days. Here," she said, trying to hand him the snake carcasses.

"No, ma'am. Me and snakes don't like each other."

She laughed. "Know what you mean." She returned them to the saddle and gave a dramatic shiver. "If it didn't make our grumpy foreman so happy, I'd have left these for the buzzards."

"Why you limpin'? Did one of them snakes bite cha?"

She bit the inside of her cheek to keep from grinning. If one of these snakes had bitten her, even through her heavy boots, she wouldn't just be in a bad mood. She wouldn't have made it all the way back to the ranch walking.

Pedro had come to the ranch on a work-release program four years ago but he'd grown up in Kansas City. His abhorrence of anything dealing with snakes was, unfortunately, a continued source of jokes from the other hands, with a multitude of rubber snakes showing up in various places around the ranch.

In a joint program with the Whispering Springs Police Department, the Flying Pig Ranch had agreed to take nonviolent teenage offenders to work off minor offenses, paying the police department for the man labor. Marti's grandfather had started the program when he'd served as Chief of Police, while still a rancher in need of hands. Over the years, hundreds of teens had mucked out stalls, brushed horses, and even helped with feeding the livestock.

Busted for selling marijuana at fourteen, Pedro had been one of those nonviolent offenders and was sent to the ranch. Hostile when he'd first arrived, he'd found his home and calling among the ranch's animals.

"No snake bites," Marti said. "Rascal has a stone bruise and possibly a slight sprain from stepping in one of the gopher holes. I didn't want him to do any further injury. I, on the other hand, fell into a hole when one of these snakes decided he wanted to strike out. His mistake. Shot his head off."

Pedro kicked his left foot free of the stirrup then bent to hold out his hand. "Climb on, and I'll give you a ride back."

"Appreciate the offer, but I can barely stand on my left leg. No way can I lift myself." She tossed him Rascal's reins. "Take Rascal on back. I'll walk."

He hesitated, and then said, "It don't seem right, leaving you here." He swung off the horse with an ease that showed years of riding. She smiled. He'd changed so much since the first time he'd tried to dismount from a horse and, instead, fell off.

"Now, don't get mad at me," he warned, seconds before grabbing her around the waist and throwing her up onto his horse's back.

She gasped in surprise and grabbed for the saddle horn before swinging her right leg over the beast.

"Sorry, ma'am, but Foreman Grisham would have me muckin' stalls by myself for a month if I left you here." He collected Rascal's reins and remounted his horse behind her. "Hold on. I'll go slow."

* * *

"Don't look good to me," Marti's father said. Patrick Jenkins frowned as he turned his daughter's leg side to side.

Marti gasped. Hot, stabbing pain radiated from her ankle up her leg. She bit her lip to keep from crying out. The swelling from day one had spread downward to her toes and up to just below her knee. She'd found her grandfather's cedar wood cane and had been using it for the past four days, hoping that, with the cane supporting most of her weight, she'd be back to normal by now. "It's just a bad sprain. I'm sure," she said.

"Carla, come here and look at your daughter's leg."

Carla Jenkins entered the living room, drying her hands on a kitchen towel. "Still swollen?"

"Yup," Patrick said. "But your daughter thinks if she ignores it, it'll go away."

Carla grinned. "*Your* daughter is as bullheaded as you."

"Your daughter is sitting right here you know," Marti muttered.

Her mother kissed her forehead. "Like we could forget." Carla pressed on the front of Marti's left leg just below her knee. Her finger sank into the swollen flesh. When she released pressure, the indentation remained. "Sorry, honey, but your father's right. It's time to see a doctor."

Marti sighed and pounded the back of her head on the pillow behind her. "I hate doctors."

"I know," her mother said. "But I don't think we have a choice."

Marti held out her hand. "Fine. Fine. Hand me my phone."

Her mother give her a sidelong look and chuckled.

"No way, honey. I know you. You'll put off the appointment as long as possible. I'll make the call."

Marti swallowed a couple of acetaminophens and gave up the fight. She knew when she was beat.

To no one's surprise, her mother pulled strings and got Marti an appointment at Riverside Orthopedic clinic for that afternoon. Marti didn't grouse too much. The last time Marti had gone out with the girls, she'd heard about a hot new doctor at that clinic. Couldn't remember the name. Didn't really matter anyway. She'd probably end up with the Physician Assistant.

After some fast talking, she convinced her parents that she could drive herself since it was her left leg that had the sprain. Her right was perfectly fine to push the brake and gas pedals.

At four o'clock, she parked outside a three-story building. She stubbornly opted to leave her grandfather's cane in the car, not wanting to even suggest she was badly injured. A mistake on her part. Walking without the cane was excruciating. With each weight-baring step, searing-hot pain shot up her left leg, making her hobble her way across the parking lot. By the time she made it into the building, up one floor to the medical clinic, and stood in front of the receptionist, her head and jaw ached from clenching her teeth.

"Good afternoon," the receptionist said. "You're limping."

Marti grabbed a tissue from the box on the counter and dabbed at the sweat on her forehead. "No kidding." She shook her head. "Sorry. It hurts."

The reception pulled out some papers and clipped them to a board. "How bad's the pain?"

"On a scale of one to ten, about fifteen." She lacked words to adequately describe what she was feeling, but *fucking hell* seemed the closest. She decided to keep that to herself.

The receptionist winced in sympathy. "Ouch. It won't be long." The reception pushed the papers toward Marti. "Fill these out. Be sure to sign here and here." She pointed to the relevant places.

After completing paperwork and waiting twenty minutes, she was taken to an x-ray room. Marti was pretty sure the young technician was a sadist. That could be the only rationale for how many times and ways her foot and ankle were positioned for pictures.

Finally, she was allowed to limp down a hall and into an exam room. She collapsed into a chair, her leg throbbing.

"Oh, I'm sorry," said the nurse, who looked about twelve years old. "I should have told you to have a seat on the table."

After a long sigh, Marti transferred to the table.

"Excellent," the child-nurse said. "Dr. Boone will be here in just a minute."

The door closed and Marti sagged against the wall. She suspected her sprained ankle might be in worse shape than she wanted to admit.

Dr. Boone? Was that the name Delene had said? Maybe, but Marti had been a few beers in that night and the name her friend had spoken could have been Johnson for all she remembered.

She waited what seemed like forever, but was probably about five minutes, before a tall, dark-haired man stepped into the room, his long white lab coat flapping around his knees.

"Sorry for the wait." He held out a hand. "I'm Elias Boone."

Marti hoped he didn't note the fact her jaw fell just a

fraction as she reached out to shake his hand. "Marti Jenkins."

He had to be the good-looking doctor Delene had gushed about because, holy moly, he was gorgeous. Dark-haired. Chocolate eyes that made her melt. Broad shoulders that stretched his white doctor coat tight. Totally yummy.

He rolled a stool over and sat. "So, Ms. Jenkins, how long have you been walking around on this ankle?"

She shut her eyes with a shake of her head, embarrassed to admit how stubborn she'd been. "Four days."

"Well, that must have been painful," he said. "Let's take a look, shall we?" He rolled the stool backwards to a computer hanging on the wall, tapped on some keys and pulled up the digital x-rays of her foot. One keystroke and the picture flashed on the wall monitor. He pointed to the monitor. "See right here?"

She leaned closer but it looked exactly like the skeleton she'd played with in her high school biology class.

"That's your ankle."

"Is it broken?" she asked with a wince.

"Today's your lucky day. It doesn't appear to be. If it is, it's only a small crack, small enough we can't see it."

Marti frowned, feeling irritated that she'd made the trip to town just to be told what she already knew. "So what you're telling me is all I have is a sprained ankle."

Despite her grumpy tone, he smiled, and she felt as though she'd been hit upside the head. That smile should carry a warning.

"I wouldn't say it's just a sprained ankle. You have what's known as a Grade 2 ankle sprain."

She blew out a breath. "English, Dr. Boone."

His mouth twitched. "It's a partial tear in your calcaneofibular ligament."

"Yikes, if that's English, then let's try French."

He laughed and a small area behind her navel tugged.

"Sorry," he said, shaking his head. "You do have a partially torn ligament. With an ankle sprain, the ligaments are stretched when the person falls or twists the foot. Sometimes, the ligaments can be stretched to the point they tear a little or even tear in half. In your case, you have a small tear. That must have been quite a twist. If I understand the story correctly, you were in a fight with a rattlesnake?"

"Nothing that brave," she answered with a chuckle. "He bared his fangs to strike and I flailed backwards, out of his way and landed in a gopher hole."

He shook his head. "I have to admit that's a different slant on how to sprain an ankle. It's usually cheerleading, or basketball, or some activity that requires moving from side to side. So no cheerleading, huh?" He grinned.

"Yeah, no. Those days are long behind me."

"Hmm."

She gave him a sideways glance. "What does that mean?"

"Just trying to picture you in a cheerleading outfit."

A loud laugh burst from her. "Not going to happen, Doc."

He smiled. Her gut tugged again. He had a beautiful smile. Full of white teeth and a pair of dimples. If she'd run into him at Leo's Bar, she'd have figured out a way to make sure they met. But in this situation, she didn't want to like him too much. She was pretty darn sure she wasn't going to like where this appointment was headed.

"Well, I have to admit a rattlesnake story is a first for me. I didn't see many rattlesnakes during my ortho residency."

"Where you from?"

"New York."

"And you moved from New York to Whispering Springs, Texas? Why would any sane person do that?"

He laughed again.

And that tug pulled again, almost taking her breath. His brown eyes sparkled with delight. Whew. Wait until the single ladies of Whispering Springs saw those eyes. Catfights would abound.

Not the time and not the place, she warned herself. Her engagement had ended badly six months ago. She wasn't looking for another guy in her life. She'd sit on the sidelines, eat her popcorn, and watch the others slug it out over him.

Too bad, though. He did make her heart sigh.

"I'll be here for the next four months while Dr. Kelley does a fellowship in knees. Apparently, people in this town blow out knees regularly."

She snorted. "Oh yeah. Working cowboys and ex-rodeo cowboys. Hard on the body."

"Now, about you..."

Sighing, she frowned. "Yeah, about me."

"You are a very lucky lady. Nothing broken, but you'll need to rest your ankle for it to heal properly."

"For how long?"

"Not horribly long. Maybe three weeks. Four at the worst."

"I have to be off my feet for three to four weeks?" She immediately began shaking her head. "Nope. No can do. I'm a rancher. My parents are leaving on their dream vacation. I can't lie around for a month. Do you have another option?"

"For a Grade 2 sprain, I usually recommend an air cast. Light. Removable for showers."

There was a knock on the door, and a woman's head popped around the corner. "Need me?"

"In a minute, Debbie."

The door shut and he paused. "What was I saying? Oh right. Air cast. It'll make walking easier, but you'll still want to baby that ankle. Rest, elevation, and ankle exercises should fix you up in no time. I'll have my nurse come back and go over some dorsiflexion-plantar-flexion range-of-motion exercises I want you to do at night."

"Great. No problem."

"Rancher. Is that what you said you did?"

She nodded.

"Your problem will be riding a horse for the next couple of weeks. Even though your foot is in a stirrup, your leg hanging down like that will cause your ankle to swell. So, I suggest you stay off horses for a couple of weeks. Is that doable?"

"I can take the ATV when I need to go into the pasture."

She would have sworn he rolled his eyes.

"Yeah," he said. "Don't do that either. Try to keep off your feet unless necessary."

"Will I need crutches?"

"I don't see the need. The air cast will support your ankle. If you still have a great deal of pain after a week to ten days, call me."

She'd love to call him but not because she was in pain.

And, she reminded herself, he was firs her doctor, and second, she wasn't looking.

But if she were...

She blew out a long, frustrated sigh. This sucked. She had two new juvenile offenders coming out on Monday as part of the joint program. She'd assumed responsibility for the program and its teens last year from Dad. The last thing she wanted was to disappoint him by being unable to do her job.

Damn gophers.

"Fine. Fine," she muttered. "Whatever."

"I'll send my nurse in with all the instructions. I know I'm throwing a lot of information at you, but everything is written down. Call me if you need anything." He squeezed her knee. "Good luck."

There was nothing sexual about the touch. It was a doctor comforting a distressed patient but her heart shot off in a gallop nonetheless.

Nope, nope, nope. She would not be attracted to a short-timer, especially a Yankee.

Two

Eli Boone closed the door to the exam room and leaned against it for a moment. When he'd agreed to see a last-minute patient as a favor to his scheduler, he'd had no idea his world would turn upside down.

He hadn't had a date since moving to Texas. A couple of sexual hook-ups, yes. Dates? No.

When Hank Kelly had asked him to come to Whispering Springs, he'd warned Eli about small-town gossip. "Watch out for the gossip grapevine," Hank had said. "And no local hook-ups, unless you want a shotgun wedding."

Eli had laughed, but Hank had added, "Trust me on this. Drive on into Dallas if you're looking for...temporary companionship. The women in Whispering Springs are great, don't get me wrong. But all the ones I know are looking for the gold band and white picket fence."

Eli had had the gold band, but instead of a white picket fence, he and his wife had had a twentieth-floor apartment in Manhattan. When Gina had died, he'd kept it for a while, but finally he'd sold. Just too many memories.

So, no, he wasn't looking for a gold band, white picket fence, or shotgun wedding. The couple of hook-ups he'd had in Dallas had left him feeling empty and unsatisfied. For now, he had a close and loving relationship with his right hand.

However, Marti Jenkins, with her laugh and that mischievous twinkle in her eye, made him wish he could get to know her a little better. She intrigued him. The first woman to do so in forever.

He pushed off the door and turned Marti over to his nurse. It was better that he move on to other duties. Lust for a patient was a complete no-no.

He headed up one floor to physical therapy. Looking around, he had to admit that his old classmate had put together a first-class facility. The first floor housed a pharmacy, administrative offices, a small café and a heated pool for therapy. The second floor held all the diagnostic services, clinic and treatment rooms, and private offices for the physicians. And finally, the top level was completely utilized by physical therapy activities. It was a very sweet setup.

The physical therapy area was in full swing. Therapists worked with clients on mats, weights, rolling balls, stationary bikes, and various other devices of torture, as the patients called them. Sitting off to one side in a wheelchair was a sandy-haired teen, Joe Manson.

Last year, Joe had broken the state record in the one-hundred-yard dash. Twenty-four hours later, he'd been riding shotgun with three friends when a drunk driver hit them head-on. Two of the four boys had been killed instantly. One had walked away with cuts and bruises. Joe's legs had been amputated in the metal wreckage, one above the knee and one below the knee. Actually, he was lucky to be alive, but he didn't see it that way. Most days, he let everyone know that he wished he'd died.

"Joe," Eli called, walking across the room to the teen. "How's it going?"

"I'm alive," Joe said with scowl. "Not my choice."

Eli decided to not comment on the attitude. "I've been reviewing your chart. You've made incredible progress. Lucky for you, teens heal quicker than adults. You were in superb condition before the accident. That's also helped the speed of your recovery."

Joe shrugged. "My superb condition didn't do shit for me. I'm still a pathetic cripple."

"Yeah, aren't you tired of that?"

Joe's head jerked. "You calling me a cripple?"

Eli shrugged nonchalantly. "Hey, apparently that's what you want to be."

Joe's eyebrows lowered in a threat. "If I could get out of this chair, I'd kick your ass."

Eli leaned close. "Oh yeah? Then get out of that chair and do it."

"You're a bastard, Dr. Boone." Joe swept his arm across the stumps that used to be his legs. "How the hell do you propose I do that, asshole? Walk on my stumps?"

"No, I propose you learn to walk on artificial legs—unless you like the idea of riding around in a chair the rest of your life. Given that you're only sixteen, you've got a long life ahead." He gave Joe a pass on the cussing. Hell, truth to tell, he'd probably be as angry as this kid. Life sucked sometimes.

The teen scoffed. "Right. Like any girl is going to date a guy with fake legs."

This time, Eli scoffed. "Give me a break. I guess you haven't noticed that we've been fighting a war for over a decade. Many of our brave men and women who once would have died due to their injuries now make it home missing a leg or arm or more. Many of them have found love and families and great lives. In fact, I read a story just the other day about a double amputee being sworn in as a new deputy with the Whispering Springs Sheriff's Department. So, if all these other folks have learned to walk, run, and have families, how are you so special that you can't, too? Or do you enjoy being... What was it you said?" He snapped his fingers. "Oh yeah. A pathetic cripple."

Joe's face reddened in anger. "Fuck you." He grabbed the wheels of his chair to roll away.

Eli grabbed the chair's handles to stop the teen from leaving. "Let me help you. I can. Before I came here, I did years of work with amputees."

The teen's whole body sagged. "You don't understand."

"Try me."

For a minute, the kid said nothing, just stared at the floor. Then he met Eli's gaze. "I was somebody. All the guys envied me. I could date any girl I wanted. There wasn't anything I couldn't do." He shook his head. "Now, I can't even stand up to take a piss."

"That's where you're wrong." Eli pulled a rolling stool over and sat. He hated when people stood over him to talk. It always made him feel diminished somehow, which was why he always sat in treatment rooms when he interacted with patients. "You can stand and piss if you want. You can walk, if you want. In fact, you can run again. But all that is up to you."

The teen grimaced. "I hate those fake legs."

Eli nodded. "Yeah, I'm glad we've gotten past the wooden peg leg too."

Joe looked at him, and for the first time, laughed. "You're crazy."

Eli grinned. "Seriously, the new legs we have today are incredible. Of course you'll have to learn how to walk on new legs, but you're young and healthy. Your muscle tone is still excellent. How about this? When's your next physical therapy appointment?"

"Wednesday."

"How about I let you talk to some of the war vets who live here and have faced exactly what you're facing? They can tell you the real truth instead of you getting all your information from a two-legger." He pointed to his own legs. When Joe hesitated, Eli added, "Do this for me. If you decide to stay on wheels instead of prosthetics after you talk to some fellow amputees, I won't bug you about it again. Your decision."

The teen was too young to spend the next sixty years in a chair, especially since there was no need. Eli knew some very persuasive vets. If he couldn't get Joe up, then those vets could.

* * *

WHEN ELI ARRIVED at the third floor the following Wednesday, Joe was surrounded by five amputees. Four of them were vets. One of the guys had lost a leg in a motorcycle accident. Eli had asked him to come because he figured Joe would identify with the accident.

But it wasn't just Joe caught up in the men's conversation. Many of the other physical therapy patients listened as they worked out replaced knees or rehabbed from some other surgery. The therapy center was loud, laughter mixing with groans and grunts.

Joe's face was a combination of awe, fear, and—maybe

for the first time—hope. The motorcycle rider had his wallet out, showing pictures of his new baby. Not to be outdone, a couple of vets were waving their pictures and bragging about their children.

Yes, this was what Joe needed to see. Normalcy. Men having great lives, great wives, children, jobs, and hobbies. He needed to understand that life went on—with or without his legs—and it was up to him to grab on and ride it like the badasses standing around him.

One of the vets announced he was late and had to get home before his wife hid his leg as punishment. Joe looked stunned. The other guys cracked up. Then comprehension dawned on Joe's face and he laughed.

While they were saying their goodbyes, Eli checked with the head of the physical therapy unit to see whether there was anything that needed his attention. There wasn't, which made Eli free for the afternoon.

Joe was still smiling when Eli rolled the stool over.

"What'd you think?" Eli asked

"Did you know there's sort of an amputee club in Whispering Springs? I mean, it's not a formal club, but the guys get together and do things?"

Eli nodded. "Yup. There are some excellent resources in this town. For example, did *you* know there's a nearby ranch that specializes in working with vets who are dealing with post-traumatic stress disorder?"

Joe shook his head. "Man, that's kind of cool."

"It is. It's owned by a military vet and his wife."

"You been there?"

Eli shook his head then leaned closer. "I'll tell you a secret. I am terrified of horses."

Joe's eyes widen and his mouth gaped in astonishment. "You're kidding. I love to ride." His face fell as his body sagged. "Well, I used to love to ride."

Eli's heart went out to the boy. "Now, don't hold me to this. I'll have to do some homework, but I'm pretty sure you can still ride. Nothing about being a double amputee stops that." He smiled. "Want me to check it out?"

"Yes!" Joe said, his eyes misting a bit.

"I'll do that for you—*if* you'll give the prosthetic legs a serious try."

Joes gave him a crooked smile. "Oh, I'd already decided to do that."

"Perfect. I'll get moving on that for you." He began to rise.

Joe reached out to stop him. "But I want you to do something for me."

Eli nodded and lowered back to the stool. "If I can, sure."

"I've done the reading, and I know it's going to take this summer to get good on my new legs."

"That sounds about right, but the prosthetist will be able to tell you more."

"I know, but while I'm learning to walk, I want you to learn to ride horses."

Eli's stomach dropped. "Excuse me?"

"Man, you're missing the best high. Being on a horse, racing through the pastures is the coolest thing ever. You can't live in Texas and not know how to ride a horse."

Eli pushed a smile onto his face. "I don't know, Joe. I'm only going to be here a few more months."

Joe laughed. "So you're telling me that I can learn to wear fake legs, learn to walk, run and even ride a horse but you, with two good legs, can't learn just one of those things?"

His heart pounding against his chest, Eli said, "I'll think about it."

Joe raised an eyebrow. "Yeah? You promise?"

"I promise."

Did a promise count if he crossed his fingers at the same time?

* * *

MARTI HAD BEEN on her air cast for a whopping four days and was already sick of it. Oh, she could walk just fine. And the pain was getting better, but she hated that the stupid air cast presented a damaged image to her ranch hands. You'd think she'd broken her back and was paralyzed the way her family and ranch hands treated her. Someone was always handing her stuff or asking how she was doing.

Argh. She'd had enough.

But it was Friday, so maybe tomorrow she could get away from all the caring eyes for a while.

She was still using her grandfather's cane occasionally to stabilize herself, and keep as much weight off her ankle as she could. From what the nurse had explained, and from online research she'd done, keeping her full, one-hundred and thirty-five pounds off her ankle could help the speed with which it healed. Heaven knew, she wanted to be back to normal as soon as possible.

She pushed up from the chair in her bedroom, established a good balance, and made her way down the stairs to the kitchen and a cup of coffee with her name on it.

"Oh, honey. What are you doing down here?" her mother exclaimed. "I would have brought you coffee." She held up the walkie-talkie on the counter. "All you had to do was ask."

"I didn't want to ask," Marti said through clenched

teeth. "I've been looking at the walls in my room for days. I've got to get outside or go crazy."

Her mother laughed. "Please. Days? You spent yesterday in your room, but only because I hid your air cast. You shouldn't be going out to the barn or the pastures. You need to spend another day in your room resting."

"No way, no how. I need to get down to the barn. Check on the new calves. And we've got those two teens from the Whispering Springs Police Department program starting. I need to make sure everything is ready."

Her mother shook her head. "You don't have to do everything around here, you know."

Marti sat at the table and rolled her eyes up to where her mother stood. "I know, but with you and Dad planning to take the summer to travel, you need to know you're leaving the ranch in good hands."

Her mother hugged her. "We know we are. You don't have anything to prove to us. Besides, we don't leave for a few more days, and we can delay the trip, if we need to."

"Absolutely not," Marti said. "You won't have to. My ankle's already feeling so much better."

"We'll see," her mother said, raising a brow.

After a quick breakfast, Marti climbed onto the ATV parked at the back door and rode it down to the barn. Any other morning, she would have walked, but Dr. Boone—the scorching-hot Dr. Boone—had stressed, as had his nurse, that she should put as little weight as possible on her ankle to help the healing. She wasn't supposed to be on a horse, dangling legs and all, but that didn't mean she couldn't help out with the daily barn chores.

She checked in with the ranch foreman and took over the grooming that needed to be done. Pedro was reassigned from grooming horses to literally shoveling shit from the stalls. The job switch was met with groans and protests, but he winked at Marti as he left Rascal's stall.

She was just laying out her combs and brushes when the foreman called her back to the barn office.

"You've got a call," he said, handing her the receiver.

"Hello?"

"Martha? This is Dr. Boone. I wanted to see how you were getting along with the boot."

His deep voice jabbed her gut, making her pull in her abdomen in response.

"Call me Marti," she said. "I'm doing fine. Swelling's down. Pain's better. Overall, I think I'll be back to normal before you know it."

"That's great. Good to hear. I, um, like to check on my patients to make sure they're doing okay."

"I am. Thank you for calling." She paused. "Is there anything else?"

She crossed her fingers this call was a ruse to ask her out. What woman wouldn't want to be seen with the attractive new doctor in town? Not a relationship sort of thing. She didn't need the hassles that went with those, but some male attention would be welcome. After all, her handheld shower massager was beginning to show signs of excessive wear and tear.

"Well, now that you ask, I wonder if I might drop by and discuss a project with you."

"A project?" Her fingers uncrossed.

Damn it. Why did she seem to draw the attention of men who needed something from her? Besides sex, she amended.

"I..." She hesitated. "Sure, why not?"

"Great. This afternoon work? About four?"

"Sure," she repeated. "See you then."

She went back into Rascal's stall, picked up a

grooming brush and began running it along the horse's side.

"So," she said to Rascal. "Guess who I just talked to?"

He shook his mane, which she interpreted as, "Tell me more."

"Dr. Hottie." A ripple ran along Rascal's back, which could have been the brush, or maybe Rascal had a sense of exactly how sexy the doctor was.

"Oh," a suspiciously Hispanic male voice said through the wall from the next stall. "I bet he wants to kiss you." This statement was followed by loud kissing noises and a girl's giggle.

"I don't know, Rascal," she said, playing along. "But I know one thing. Pedro is going on the mucking list for the rest of the week if I see him in the next two minutes."

"This isn't Pedro," the voice said. "This is Rascal." The girl's giggle leaked through the stall's wall.

Marti rolled her eyes. Her latest police department offenders were a couple of seventeen-year-old girls who'd been caught throwing toilet paper into the trees in the high school yard. They'd been sentenced to the ranch for a month of stall mucking.

"Uh-huh. Now that I'm done with you, Rascal, I'll be moving to Jack's stall." She dragged her feet in the straw to make extra noise as she moved toward the door.

She heard four feet shuffling hurriedly in the next stall, the creak of Jack's stall door, and pounding as Pedro and one of the girls ran for the exit. Still, she couldn't keep from grinning. Hot Doc was coming, even if he had an agenda. It was possible his "project" was an excuse to see her.

She didn't know, but that sounded so much better to her ego.

About three, she called it a day and headed up to the

house. She stepped into the outdoor shower, securing the door behind her. After a day covered in manure, dirt, blood, and a number of unidentifiable splotches, she was glad to shuck her clothes for a shower. She rolled up everything and shoved it through the chute into the laundry room.

Years ago, her mother had gotten tired of the smells and muck that came in on her husband's clothes. For Christmas one year, she'd requested a shower that could be accessed from the outside and adjacent to her laundry room. Of course, the various odors still filled her laundry room when the clothes went through the chute, but she'd assured him the addition was exactly what she'd wanted, keeping the various ranch aromas from the rest of the house.

As the warm water sluiced down her body carrying away the evidence of her day, Marti decided her mother was one intelligent woman. Now that she was keeping house and doing her own clothes, she appreciated the idea of having a home that didn't smell like the barn.

After wrapping herself in a towel, she opened the door that led to an interior hall and made her way to her bedroom. She wasn't putting on fresh clothes because of Dr. Boone. She would have done this even if her afternoon visitor had been old man Hopkins.

Right, Marti. No one would be fooled with that story, especially herself.

A little before four, she poured a glass of wine, grabbed the latest Cattlemen Magazine and snapped it open to a pasture management article. It didn't hold her interest. She tossed the glossy magazine on the sofa and picked up today's paper to do the crossword. That would distract her, not that she was anxious about seeing Dr. Boone.

At ten minutes past four, her cell phone buzzed. The screen readout was Riverside Orthopedics. Ah. He was running late. How like a doctor.

"Hello?"

"Martha Jenkins?" a female voice asked.

"Yes."

"Ms. Jenkins. This is Debbie Watts from Riverside Ortho. Dr. Boone asked that I call and let you know that he was called into emergency surgery and wouldn't be able to keep the appointment for this afternoon."

"Oh." The bottom dropped out of Marti's heart. "Well, I guess these things happen."

"All the time," the nurse said.

"Thank you for the call."

"Sure thang."

Well, shoot. Here she was on a Friday night, all cleaned up with nowhere to go. No use letting all this makeup go to waste.

Two calls later and she was meeting Delene Younger and Tina Baker at Leo's Bar and Grill for some dinner, drinking, and—bum ankle or not—dancing. Oh, and she might throw in a little Dr. Hottie gossip just for Delene.

Three

Saturday morning, Marti woke with a pounding headache, throbbing to the beat of the country song blasting on her alarm. Groaning, she rolled to her side and put a pillow over her head. Right now, being a Monday-through-Friday office worker seemed like the ideal job, and she didn't even know what an office worker did. It just had to be better than getting up at the crack of dawn on a weekend with a hangover.

Of course, the reality was that ranchers didn't have weekends. They worked seven days a week.

When her second alarm went off at five a.m., time for lounging around in bed was done. Cattle liked breakfast as much as she did.

Later that morning, she saw her parents off on their summer trip, after swearing and crossing her heart that she would call if anything came up. While she was crossing her heart, she was also crossing her fingers. It would take a problem of massive magnitude before she interrupted their trip. They had worked hard their whole lives and deserved some fun.

Throughout the day, she kept her cell phone with her, expecting Eli Boone to call and reschedule, maybe even apologize for having to cancel their...what was it anyway? Date? Appointment? Whatever it was supposed to be, he didn't call and reschedule—not for that night, not for tomorrow, not for anytime.

Ranching meant early hours, with some late nights not unusual. Her evening was penciled in for early bed and a good book. So, she told herself, it was just as well he didn't call for today.

As the next week rolled by, the call to apologize and reschedule never came. She did get calls from Zack Marshall, a local cowboy, and Chad Jamison, a cute fireman from the city. Both asked her out for Saturday night. She'd been out with them both in the past, and while they were drop-dead handsome, she didn't feel like dressing up and heading out on a date with either.

She'd known Zack since first grade, so it was hard to not picture him without his front teeth. Besides, he had some on-and-off thing with her friend Delene.

Chad was a different story. He'd moved to Whispering Springs as an adult, so he'd always had his front teeth. But he had a complicated relationship with Tina, and Marti didn't want to get sucked into their vortex of breakups and makeups. She figured the date invite was probably an effort on his part to make Tina jealous. She wasn't interested in being a player in that play.

By the end of her parents' second week of vacation, she'd spoken with her parents every day. She told them that from now on, she would only accept their calls on Tuesdays and Thursdays. Her mother had laughed and apologized. But Marti understood. Letting go was hard for them, even if it was only for three months.

On the Monday morning of her parents' third week of

vacation, she stood sipping a cup of coffee as she studied the two hospital auxiliary fundraiser tickets stuck beneath a magnet on her refrigerator. She looked at the date on the tickets, checked the calendar on her phone, and realized the dinner-slash-dance was the coming Saturday evening, as in only five days away. Even though she'd walked past those tickets for two months, she'd let the event sneak up on her. She had no date, and to be honest, no man she wanted to ask. Delene already had tickets and none of her other girlfriends had any interest in attending a stuffy formal affair.

At two-hundred and fifty bucks a pop, she would go eat rubber chicken with or without an escort. Her grandmother had founded the auxiliary and the Jenkinses had always supported the auxiliary's work. This year, she would be the family's sole representative, so not attending wasn't an option.

Of course, it wouldn't be the first time she'd gone solo. Last May, her fiancé had been too busy to attend—with what, she only found out months later. At the time, he'd only said he had "a thing" to do with his friend Scott.

The event was black tie, and most of the guys in her dating pool would rather eat their cowboy hats than put on a tux for an evening of schmoozing and dancing. Too bad she had the perfect dress that would knock a date's eyes out. Plus, her ankle was feeling stronger, so she was taking herself out of that blasted air cast on Saturday. She'd be ready to dance again, albeit gently.

She was sure the Montgomery family would be there. They always supported events such as this. The wives were happy to share their guys on the dance floor. She could snag a dance or two that way.

Tuesday evening, just as she was exiting the shower, her cell phone rang. With water trickling down her body onto the shower mat, she considered letting it go to voicemail. It'd been a rough day. She was tired and more than a little grumpy. Still…

"Hello?"

"Marti? It's Eli Boone."

Stunned, she almost dropped the phone. She pulled the phone away and looked at the caller ID. Riverside Ortho. "Well, surprise. I thought you'd dropped off the face of the earth."

"I know, I know. After eight hours of surgery and spending the night in the hospital, I had just barely enough time to get home, grab my suitcase, and make my plane." He paused. "You did get the message about the emergency surgery?"

"I did, but that two weeks ago. Hard to believe that emergency surgery lasted that long. Must be a new surgical record."

"Darn it. Debbie was supposed to tell you I was leaving for Europe in the morning and wouldn't be back until yesterday. I attended an international symposium on bone grafting in Copenhagen."

"Can you hold on a minute?" Setting the phone on the lip of the sink, she whisked the towel over the water droplets, and then wrapped it around her and moved into her bedroom. "Sorry. I'm back. No, I didn't get that message."

He sighed. "I'm sorry. You must think I'm horrible. First, I ask for a favor and then never call."

"I've been pretty busy around here, so I honestly haven't given it much thought," she lied.

"Now I feel even worse because I need two favors."

"Really?" She sat on the edge of her bed.

"I know it's late notice, and you probably already have plans for Saturday, but I've got these two tickets for the hospital fundraiser on Saturday night. I was hoping you might go with me. It's a worthy cause. The auxiliary is trying to raise funds for some badly needed equipment."

She thought about the five-hundred-dollar tickets stuck onto her fridge. "I am aware of it, yes."

"Would you be interested in going with me? To the fundraiser, I mean."

Her breath caught as nerves quivered in her gut. As she was thinking, he added, as though it were an enticement—which it wasn't—"It'll give me a chance to talk about what I wanted last week. Plus, I'm kind of new in town. It'd be nice to have someone everyone knows with me."

He was asking her out because he could use her to introduce him around? Surprisingly, her house smoke alarms did not begin blaring from the smoke pouring from her ears.

"I'm messing this all up, aren't I?" he asked. "Let me be honest. I haven't dated in years. I married the last girl I asked out, so..." His voice drifted off.

"You're married?" she asked with a gasp.

"What? Oh no. I'm not any longer." He blew out a breath. "It's a long story. Say you'll go with me. I promise to explain everything."

Hadn't she just been lamenting her lack of a date just yesterday? And she really did hate to go alone.

"You realize it's black tie, right?"

"Tux is cleaned, pressed, and ready to go."

"And about this pesky issue of a doctor dating a patient?"

"Oh, you're not my patient any longer. I'm discharging you from my care. Shoot, I didn't even ask. How is your ankle? You said it was doing okay."

"I'm fine. Ready to dance even," she said. "I'd love to go with you."

"Great. I haven't been to your house yet, so I'm not sure how much time to allow for the drive."

"Why don't I just meet you there? It'd be easier."

"Absolutely not." He sounded aghast. "Will seven-fifteen work?"

"It'll work fine. I'll see you on Saturday."

She hung up and flopped back on her bed with a giggle. She felt like a sixteen-year-old getting asked to prom instead of a thirty-year-old being asked to a stuffy dinner.

But she did have a great dress.

* * *

ELI HUNG up the phone with a grimace. He was out of practice when it came to asking a woman on a date. His late wife had been the last person he'd asked out, and they'd both been about seventeen at the time. Damn, he'd almost blown it with the most interesting woman he'd met in a long time, like maybe eighteen years.

He missed Gina, but she'd been gone for over seven years. After her death, he'd dived headfirst into his residency. He'd stayed at the hospital almost nonstop for the first three years. The long hours, the mental grind and sheer exhaustion made time pass by in a blur.

Then, later in his residency, he'd gone to the frontlines of the war to get surgical experience with traumatic injuries. Those days had been thrilling and mind-numbingly terrifying. Occasionally, it had flittered through his mind that if he died over there, it might be okay.

But he hadn't, and he told himself it was time to move on with his life, a major factor in his decision to take this temporary position in Texas. Sure, he was helping out a classmate, but physically separating from New York City with all its memories to a house in a small town in Texas, did help with his mindset. Gina's parents had been wonderfully supportive in the years since her death, even going so far as to help him remove her clothing and shoes. But her touches in the apartment had remained.

The painting over the fireplace that she'd bought in Paris on their honeymoon.

The four million pillows she'd insisted their bed needed.

The grand piano she'd played.

Living in a place so imprinted with her memories had finally become too much for him to endure. Last year, he'd sold everything, including the apartment, and moved to his parents' place in the Hamptons. The wind, the sand, the salt air had helped piece him back together. Not the way he'd been. That man was gone. Today, he was a different man, molded from life experiences and a lot of beach time. He was ready to start over.

Of course, starting over meant back in New York City, not Whispering Springs, Texas. He'd agreed to do these six months for Hank as a favor. As soon as the position at New York Midtown Orthopedic Practice was finalized, he'd be joining the largest and most prestigious orthopedic practice in New York. He'd be back in his element, back into the societal strata he'd grown up in.

Besides, who in their right mind would turn down a partnership in such a world-renowned practice?

The rest of the week flew. Joe gave him tons of grief about horseback riding, but that dare had gotten the teen out of his chair and onto prosthetics. He was making remarkable progress, which he never failed to point out to his doctor.

What Eli hadn't said aloud was that he'd tried horseback riding at summer camp when he'd been about ten, once on his honeymoon and again a couple of years later on vacation. His late wife had ridden like she was one with the animal. Eli rode more like a melting scoop of ice cream on a hot day, slowly sliding off the side.

Eli was used to being the smartest guy in the group. As a kid, he'd been overweight and more interested in chess than athletic endeavors. His father had insisted Eli enroll in a summer camp that focused on outdoor activities like horseback riding. The camp had been the stuff of every nerdy kid's nightmares. Using intellect and reason, he could usually work through any problem—until it came to horses. His horse anxiety and his lack of ability to overcome it had been a tough pill to swallow.

By the time he'd reached high school, he'd lost his baby fat, gotten contacts, and learned he was pretty good at running, earning a spot on the high school track team. But he'd never forgotten being the tormented fat kid. Only the new girl in school saw him for how he was then. Gina had only known the tall, confident track star with brains. He'd liked that about her. Their history hadn't encompassed those painful years.

He wished he hadn't even raised the horse issue with Joe, who was like a dog with a bone on the topic. Still, he found ways to put off the teen each time he asked about Eli's progress with riding. But the time was quickly approaching when he'd be forced to admit he hadn't done anything about the dare. That might be misconstrued by Joe that his doctor had been bullshitting him all along. That would certainly drive a serious wedge in the doctor-patient relationship.

Saturday came, and Eli found himself unexpectedly nervous about the date. Marti had been released as a patient, so it wasn't as if he were breaking any medical tenet. Still, it'd been a while, and dating in high school had been easy compared to dating as an adult.

The drive to the Flying Pig Ranch took about five minutes longer than he'd planned. Since he'd left early, he arrived in plenty of time, but thank goodness for GPS. He might never have found his way along the unpaved back roads.

He turned and drove between the ranch's gateposts. The drive was dirt and limestone gravel, and his car's tires threw up both behind him. His first view of her house was exactly what his mind had envisioned: a two-story, white-stone traditional ranch with a wraparound porch, complete with a couple of rockers and ferns hanging in pots.

Climbing from his SUV, he immediately noticed the aroma of sage and cedar that gave the air a freshly clean scent. He drew in a deep breath. His mother paid a fortune to housekeepers to get this fresh smell in the family home.

Horses in the corral nickered as they studied the new arrival, probably judging him inadequate. In the distance, a barn that appeared freshly painted stood with entrance doors securely closed, but a smaller one in the loft stood open.

On the other side of the house, a large pasture that looked to go on forever held various groupings of brown cows. Most of the cattle had settled down in the grass for the night. An owl hooted from somewhere. A light breeze made the leaves rustle. Peaceful, but not quiet.

Turning back to the horses, he studied them. They were beautiful creatures, no doubt about that. However, the thought of being on the back of one sent chills down his spine. The horrible memories of summer camp came rushing back. First time on a horse, he'd found himself flat on his back after falling off. The counselors had assured him the horse had taken only a couple of steps, but Eli called bullshit. That horse had bucked him off. Of course, falling off a horse that basically wasn't moving made Eli the target of lots of cruel jokes.

The next summer, he'd convinced his parents to send him to band camp, not that he was great with his saxophone. But at least he wasn't the butt of all the jokes.

By high school, most of the geekiness stayed in his past.

Maybe he should just admit that he might be a great doctor, but would never be even an adequate rider.

He made his way up onto the front porch and rang the bell. After a few moments, he heard the slide of a window.

"Hey, I'm up here," Marti called.

He backed off the porch and looked up. Marti looked down at him, a wide grin on her face. How could a simple smile transform her from pretty to total knockout? She appeared to be wearing a towel and not much else.

"Sorry, I'm running about ten minutes late. I had a stubborn bull who decided to jump a fence."

Eli gestured to the towel and then to his tux. "I might be a little overdressed compared to you."

She laughed, the sound ricocheting through him like a pinball.

"I'll see if I can come up with something more appropriate to wear. Door's open. Let yourself in. There's beer and wine in the kitchen—if you can find it. Bourbon, scotch and whatever in the living room. Help yourself to a drink. I swear, I won't be but just a minute."

"Or ten," he said.

She gave him a thumbs-up and disappeared back into the house.

The door was unlocked, and he entered into a gleaming clean foyer. A flight of stairs leading to the second floor stood directly in front of him. He could probably march up those and find his semi-dressed date, not that he would, but the idea of Marti only partially dressed was enticing.

The wood of the floors and walls shined under the ceiling lights. The main living room was to his right, so he wandered in there. A large fireplace dominated the room. A pair of chairs and a worn, overstuffed sofa suggested the room got a lot of use. He had no trouble believing that. He could envision a roaring fire on a cold night and snuggling on the sofa.

Now he was being ridiculous. He needed help from this woman, not snuggling on a cold night. Besides, he would be heading back to New York in only three short months, as soon as the partnership deal came through.

He sat on the sofa—comfortable as advertised—and studied the stack of magazines on the coffee table. He'd expected *People*, or *Cosmopolitan*, or some other rag directed at female readers. Instead, he leafed through *Texas Cattlemen*, *Texas Women Ranchers*, Whispering Springs' local paper and today's *Wall Street Journal*.

His brain chastised him. *Sexist much, doctor?*

He settled back to read the Wall Street Journal, but had gotten only a couple of pages in when he heard Marti's footsteps on the stairs. Dropping the newspaper back onto the table, he rose. When she entered the room, his breath caught.

Holy shit. The cowgirl was gone. In her place stood an elegant, poised woman who might grace any social event his parents attended on a regular basis. And she'd achieved the look in under ten minutes.

"Wow," he said with a gulp of air. He twirled a finger in the air. "Do a three-sixty."

Her dark auburn hair was secured in a twist at the back of her head, but curly strands hung along her face. Her dress. Damn. What could he say? Thin black straps held up a satiny-looking long, straight dress that draped around her curves. It dipped modestly in the front, but when she turned away from him, his heart leapt at the sight she presented. The back plunged low to a vee just past her waist, leaving a luscious view of creamy, smooth skin. He gulped again.

"Wow. Just wow."

Completing the spin, she grinned. "You clean up pretty good yourself, doctor." She imitated his finger twirl. "Your turn."

He rotated in a circle then faced her again. "Sorry. Nothing tantalizing in my attire."

She picked up a small black clutch from a side table and pointed it at him. "You are so wrong. Men underestimate the power of a suit, especially a well-fitting tux. I'll be pushing my friends away from you all night."

Chuckling, he walked to where she stood. "And here I was thinking the same about you, except I don't know many people in Whispering Springs, so I'll be dueling with strangers."

A flush pinkened her cheeks. "Nicest thing I've heard in a long time. Shall we go?"

Holding out a bent arm, he said, "Let's go rock this shindig."

Four

Call her shallow, but walking into a black-tie affair on the arm of a drop-dead handsome guy beat walking in alone. As they entered the elaborate ballroom of the Grand Manor Hotel, Marti smiled and waved to a few people she knew. Eli acknowledged a couple of doctors with head tosses.

"I was right," he whispered, bending to her ear.

She liked the way his breath feathered across her cheek. "About what?" she asked, her voice breathless.

"Walking in with the hottest chick in the room on my arm does make this easier."

Her heart cartwheeled. She squeezed his arm. "And here I was thinking that being on the arm of such a handsome guy would make all my friends jealous." She waved to Delene across the room, whose eyebrows shot high. "As far as I can see, my plan is working."

He gave her a warm smile. "These poor men having to just make do with their dates after I snagged the best one."

"You know it." She laughed, not remembering a time lately when she'd last felt so carefree. Last fall's broken engagement had hit her hard, personally and emotionally. "Where are we sitting?"

Pulling a card from inside his jacket, he said, "Table five."

She arched an eyebrow. "Near the front. Now, I am impressed."

He laughed and let her lead the way toward the front of the room. After they found table five, he asked, "Can I get you a drink?"

"Please. Dirty martini."

"Brave choice." He touched her bare shoulder.

His fleeting caress stirred the lava pit of lust inside her.

"Be right back."

She set her purse on the table. There were no other patrons sitting there at the moment, but there were a couple of clutch purses, similar to hers, lying near place settings.

"Now, don't tell me we are lucky enough to have Ms. Marti Jenkins at our table," a masculine Texas voice drawled.

She turned and spun into the arms of Jason Montgomery. "Jason! What a nice surprise." She pulled his wife in for a hug. "Lydia. You look wonderful. I wondered if you'd be able to get away from the kids tonight."

Jason and Lydia had adopted her sister's children after a horrible accident took their parents' lives. Then they'd had a baby of their own within a year.

Lydia laughed. "We are so lucky to both have parents here in town. My folks have our children. Jason's folks have the rest of the Montgomery grandchildren."

"Oh my goodness," Marti said. "That'll make for a wild time at their house this evening."

"My folks love it," Jason said. "Go figure." He looked at his wife. "Drink?"

"Red wine, please."

He glanced at Marti.

"My date's bringing mine."

He wandered off toward the bar as she and Lydia were joined by Paige Montgomery, Lydia's sister-in-law, married to Cash Montgomery. Their conversation quickly drifted off to the dresses worn for the evening. The men came back carrying drinks and the three couples took their seats, which left two open seats at the table.

"Any other Montgomerys joining us?" Marti asked.

"Not that I know of," Jason said.

Cash shook his head. "Nope. The rest of them are on the other side of the room. Heaven knows I see enough of them at Sunday lunches. I don't want to see them on Saturday night, too."

The group at the table chuckled, while Jason playfully slugged Cash's arm. Shortly, a tall man with a limp and a petite lady joined the table. As one, all the men stood for the new woman.

"Gracious," she said in a thick Southern accent. "I'm so glad the Montgomery men were taught their manners." She tapped Eli's arm. "And you, sir, where are you from?"

"New York, ma'am," Eli said.

"Ah, a Yankee in our midst," she replied with a grin.

"Only visiting," he assured her. "We're not invading, or at least not yet."

Her laugh was soft and gay.

Marti felt the urge to pop Dr. Cora Bell Lambert. How dare she be petite and cute!

"I believe some of you know my date. Dax Cooper. Dax, this is Marti Jenkins. She owns the ranch that backs up to the Landry place. I don't believe I know your Yankee, Marti."

Marti forced a smile on her face, but when she turned

toward Eli, the forced smile melted into a genuine one. "This is Dr. Eli Boone. He's here covering for Hank Kelley while he does something. What is it again, Eli?"

"An advanced training experience," he explained to the table.

Each man retook his seat once Cora Bell was seated.

"Not that I'm explaining anything to Dr. Montgomery or Ms. Montgomery," Eli said to Lydia and Paige, the former a physician, and the latter an advanced practice nurse. "You are both aware that keeping up with medical advances is tough."

Both women acknowledged his comment with a nod.

"Very aware," Dr. Lydia Henson-Montgomery said. "I'm doing a six-week advanced training on burns later this year. How much longer will Hank be gone?"

"Just three months. The course was an intensive six-month program. When I talked to him last, he was exhausted. Said he might want to take a couple of additional weeks off at the end before he comes back." Eli shrugged. "Fine with me if he does. Things here are flowing nicely."

Talk turned away from medicine and on to the weather, as safe a topic as can be and one that held the attention of all the ranchers and farmers in the area. Rubber chicken was served and consumed, along with bottles of red and white wine to help wash it down. The cheesecake held no appeal, so Marti passed it off to Eli.

"No cheesecake?" he asked with astonishment.

"I've eaten my horse's weight in that stuff. I'm over it."

Eli ate his piece and hers, and then moaned. "Shouldn't have done that. I'll have to add a couple of extra miles to my jog tomorrow."

"You want to start that exercise program tonight?"

Marti asked with a tilt of her head toward the dance floor. "Music's starting."

Eli shoved back his chair and held out a hand. "Trip the light fantastic with me?"

"Man. That's an old one."

"Blame my grandmother," he said with a laugh. "She loved to dance."

Grasping his hand, she stood. "Lead on."

His hand was broad, and thick, and very warm. Her breath caught at the touch of his hand. Her heart galloped across her chest. She licked her lips nervously. Luckily for her, he was leading her to the dance floor so his back was toward her, and he couldn't see her reaction to his touch. Once on the floor, he twirled her and caught her with a hand at her waist. Holy crap.

Eli was a smooth dancer, guiding her around the floor with a polished ease that hinted at either hours of dances or formal instruction. She wasn't sure which, maybe both. Interestingly, she wasn't surprised at how he danced. Everything about the way he carried himself and spoke to others hinted at an exclusive—meaning wealthy —background.

But if that was true, why was he here in this podunk little town? She loved Whispering Springs, but she grew up here and knew all the town's secrets. What did her town look like through the eyes of an outsider? Not just a person from outside Whispering Springs, but from outside of Texas?

When the first slow song began, he pulled her flush to his body and she completely lost her train of thought. He wrapped his arm around her waist, settling his hot fingers against the flesh uncovered by the deep vee design of the dress's back. Her insides melted as lust pooled low in her gut.

If he could do that with a touch, heaven help her if he kissed her. She might go up in flames.

They swayed to the music, her head resting on a broad shoulder. His masculine scent filled her nose as she drew in a deep breath. His cologne was a spicy aroma she'd never smelled on a man. But then, wasn't it true that how a cologne smelled on one man might be different on another because of body chemistry? Whatever the reason, the scent blended with all his oozing testosterone to make her dizzy with lust.

As the song came to an end, he leaned her into a deep dip. When he pulled her up, he hugged her, then released her, much to her disappointment. "How about some fresh air?"

Before she could answer, a male voice said, "Well, I'm surprised you'd show your face at this event."

Marti's heart dropped. "Hello, Mr. Roth."

Eli's arm wound around her shoulder and he eased her closer.

"Your grandmother would be so ashamed that you'd sully her event by coming." He made the comment with his nose so high in the air, Marti could almost count his nose hairs.

"Sir—" Eli started.

Marti stopped him with a gentle elbow in his side.

"My grandmother was my greatest champion, as I am hers. She would be proud that I'm here representing the Jenkins family."

Roth scoffed. "I notice your parents aren't here. Probably still embarrassed by you. Of course, it's their fault you've turned out the way you have."

Roth's wife tugged at his arm. "That's enough, Teddy. Let's go."

"Yes, *Teddy*," Eli said with a sneer. "That really is enough."

Roth looked at Eli. "I hear you're a respectable man with an excellent future. Don't waste it on a whore like this." He gave Marti the evil eye and walked away with his wife, who looked over her shoulder and mouthed, "I'm sorry."

Marti nodded and turned to Eli, mustering a determined smile. "A breath of fresh air sounds perfect right now."

Eli's face was a mask of fury.

She tugged on his arm to get him away from the Roths before a more public confrontation occurred. "Let's go."

The ballroom had doors leading to an exterior terrace littered with tables and chairs and benches. They were not the first to escape the overheated room.

Eli laced his fingers through hers and led her off to a solo bench in the shadows. Once there, he put his finger under her chin and lifted her face.

"I don't know what that was all about, but I think that man needs to see a psychiatrist," he said—and then pressed his mouth to hers.

The kiss was a light touch of lips. Nothing over the top or too intense, perfect for calming her embarrassment of the situation.

"I'm proud to be seen with you, regardless of what that ass said. Thank you for coming with me tonight."

Marti rested her head on his hard chest. "I'm so sorry for Teddy Roth. I didn't expect him to be here this year. He's done a pretty good job of avoiding anything that has to do with my family."

"Whatever his beef is, that outburst was inappropriate."

She looked at Eli's beautiful face and sighed. She sat on the bench and pulled him down next to her.

"Last fall, I was engaged to be married to Theodore Roth, their son. Obviously, the wedding didn't happen."

"You don't have to explain," Eli said. "I'm not here to pass judgment."

"No, I want to. Really." Her hands squeezed into fists.

He lifted the hand closest to him, uncurled the fingers, and kissed the palm.

Butterflies flittered in her stomach. This man was much too polished for a rough cowgirl like her. She wanted to jerk away, sure her work-roughed hands would be a turn-off. She didn't, but she swore to do more hand care treatment in the future.

"Take your time or say never mind. It's totally up to you."

She drew a deep breath. "About a week before the wedding, I went to Theodore's condo in town to drop off some presents. He wasn't expecting me, but I had a key, so no big deal. I thought I'd let myself in and lock up when I was done." She paused.

"Let me guess," Eli said. "He wasn't alone."

She nodded slowly. "He wasn't, but the person he was with wasn't who I expected."

"Your best friend," he guessed.

"Close. His best friend, Scott. They were making love. Theodore was horrified that I'd found out. Scott was glad. They'd been lovers since their freshman year of college. They were, and are, deeply in love with each other, but Theodore knew his parents would never accept Scott." She drew in another deep breath. "I was furious at both of them. I had no interest in being Theodore's beard."

She turned to look at Eli. "I should have been more upset to find out Theodore had been unfaithful, but what

I felt was anger that I'd be duped. Theodore begged me to go through with the wedding. The Roths are quite wealthy—well, maybe filthy rich would be a better way to put it. He promised me complete control of his trust fund to marry him. I don't even know how many millions that might have been and frankly, it didn't matter. He said he'd give me all that money, and he would find a job somewhere else, so we'd be married in name only, me being a very rich wife with a husband whose job required him to live elsewhere. I, of course, would have to stay in Whispering Springs because of the ranch. Getting the picture?"

"I am," he replied in a very deep voice.

"That plan was insane. I would never marry for money. Never! Our ranch gets by. We aren't rich by any stretch of the imagination, but I don't have to eat ramen noodles for dinner every night."

"Ah, yes. The good old college days. Ramen noodles when the allowance ran short."

She grinned. "So you understand that?"

With a chuckle, he nodded.

"Anyway, the three of us—Theodore, Scott and I—talked the rest of the day and into the next day. They'd been together for years. Scott wanted to marry Theodore, who was, and probably still is, terrified of his parents' reaction to the news that he loves a man. I believe Theodore loved me, but not like he loves Scott. I could see it when he looked at the other man. The love simply poured from his eyes. It broke my heart. I wanted a man to look at me the way Theodore was looking at Scott. I couldn't hate Theodore for being in love with someone else. Hell, I'm surprised Scott didn't hate me for trying to break them up—not that I knew there was anything to break up," she added in a rush.

"Anyway," she continued, "I realized I wouldn't be

marrying Theodore, and then the awareness came to me that I wasn't *that* upset. I should have been, but I wasn't. I think I was getting married because I was twenty-nine, almost thirty, and so many of my childhood friends were married and having babies. I loved Theodore, but I wasn't in love with him. I was in love with being married. Does that make sense?"

Eli nodded. "That must have been a difficult day."

"You have no idea. Theodore begged me not to tell his folks, or anyone for that matter." She looked at Eli. "I'm only telling you because first, you got sucked into Teddy Roth's vitriolic wrath tonight, and second, you'll be leaving Whispering Springs. I trust you'll keep this under your hat."

"Of course." He put an arm around her and hugged. "They did me a great favor, you know."

"They did?"

He pressed a soft kiss to her mouth. "You are free to see me."

She smiled. "I like how you think."

Snaking an arm around his neck, she pulled him in for a long, wet kiss. Her lips parted and he slipped his tongue inside to caress hers with long strokes.

His heady scent intoxicated her as it had on the dance floor. He pulled her close, smashing her breasts against his chest with a hard tug. His hands found the naked flesh of her back in the low vee of her dress. He ran his fingers and palms across her skin, slipping fingers under the edges of the satin material.

Her heart raced and jumped with each stroke of his tongue against hers, each touch of his fingers on her back. Overcome with all the sensations, she could barely take it all in, barely catch her breath. This reaction, this complete submission of her body, was unlike anything she'd ever experienced. She was out of her league, in waters much too deep for a simple cowgirl like her.

She pulled away and dropped her forehead on his shoulder. She drew in a deep breath, willing her heart to slow, demanding the storm of emotions inside to cease. Nothing worked. A quiver rattled her, and a shiver ran down her spine.

"Are you cold?"

His deep, sensual voice did nothing to calm the emotional tempests inside her. If anything, his question fed fuel to her fires.

"No, no." She raised her head until their gazes met. "I'm fine." Her voice was a tad breathless, as though she'd just wrestle a calf to the ground for branding.

They sat in the quiet while they gathered their thoughts, and their breath.

"So, what happened to Theodore and Scott?"

She put her head against his chest, relieved to have a moment to collect herself. His heart pounded in her ear. It made her happy to know she'd caused his heart to race like hers.

"I did love Theodore, maybe not in the way I should, but I did care for him. I wanted him to have a wonderful life. Marrying me wouldn't do that. We called off the wedding. No specific reason was given, but someone started a rumor that I'd been found in bed with the best man. My money is on Theo's father, because in his mind, his son was perfect, so I had to be the guilty party." She chuckled softly. "How ironic, huh? Theodore and Scott left Texas and moved to Vermont. I talk to them often. They've married and are very happy."

She looked up at him. "Of course, his parents don't know. And although I might gossip as much as the next woman, I don't want Theodore and Scott's personal life to be fodder for the gossip mill. I wouldn't have told you, but I felt you deserved a sane explanation of that completely insane conversation you had to witness. Plus, you don't really care about the town gossip. My family knows, of course, as does my best friend. But they'll never say anything. They all know what kind of person Teddy Roth is."

With a sigh, she rested the back of her head on the stone wall behind them. "The Roths know he has a great job there and is happy. But Teddy will never forgive me for driving his son away, or at least that's his version of the story. He tells everyone that Theodore was so distressed and mortified by my indiscretion, that he left not only Whispering Springs but Texas. People in town just nod and let Teddy rant, but most pay him no mind. Maybe someday, Theodore can tell his parents about Scott, but until then, it's not my place."

"It's not fair," Eli said.

"What isn't? The Roths' reaction to Theodore leaving?"

"No. I mean, it's not fair that you have to take all the heat, while he gets off scot-free, no pun intended."

She sat up and chuckled. "I'm not worried about it. Life is good. I love where I am. I mostly feel sorry for Theodore. His mother is a wonderful lady. Sometimes, like tonight, I suspect she knows the truth and can't tell her husband. How she puts up with Teddy is a good question." Placing her hand on his chest, she said, "So that's my story. What's yours?"

"There you are," said a female voice.

Marti looked up to find her friend Delene Younger walking toward them. "You disappeared when that horrible Teddy Roth said something to you. We were all worried. Do you need me to go kick his ass for you? I will, you know."

Marti laughed and stood. Eli rose with her. "Thanks, Delene, but I'm good. Have you met Eli Boone? Eli, this is Delene Younger, one of my bestest buddies. Delene, this is Dr. Eli Boone. He's covering for Hank Kelley while he does some additional training."

Delene extended her hand. "Nice to meet you, doc. You friends with Hank?"

Eli shook her hand. "I am. Met him back in med school, and then ended up in the same residency program."

Delene whistled. "So, you're one of those fancy Harvard doctors, huh?"

Eli laughed. "Harvard, yes. Fancy, not so much."

"Where's your date?" Marti asked. "And better yet, who's your date?"

Delene rolled her eyes. "I'm here with Zack, only because I couldn't find anyone else with a tux."

"Right," Marti said. "And you probably really looked hard, huh?"

Delene gave Marti's shoulder a gentle shove. "I did look. I swear. Besides, nobody fills out a tux like Zack." She pumped her brows in an exaggerated fashion.

Marti looked at Eli, who wore a puzzled expression. "Delene and Zack dated in high school. They were the 'it' couple. Now, none of us can figure out what's going on with them."

Delene sighed. "Nothing. I needed a date. He has a tux. He wanted a free meal. Plus, he made me wash his truck today so we could bring it tonight."

Marti rolled her eyes. Beside her Eli choked back a laugh.

Delene looked over her shoulder. "I'd better get back before Zack decides to head home. You know cowboys. He wanted to leave as soon as I'd taken my last bite of cheesecake. Said it was past his bedtime, and sadly, I don't think he was kidding." She hugged Marti and said, "Call me tomorrow and we can..." She looked at Eli and back to Marti. "Gossip."

After Delene left, their little corner of the terrace seemed too quiet. "You ready to head back in?" Eli asked.

"Actually, Zack had a point. It is getting late. Maybe we should say our goodbyes and head out."

Eli checked his watch. "It's only a little after eleven."

"Eleven!" she said with a mock gasp and slapped a hand to her chest. "Why, I turn into a witch hag at midnight. Hurry."

He put his arm around her shoulders and pulled her in close. "You could never be a witch hag," he said in that low, sexy tone that melted every bone in her body.

She shivered again, not from the cold, but from the fire that flared inside her. "I haven't forgotten about your marriage. You can tell me the story later, but I can be assured you're not married now, right?"

"Marti," he said, his voice like rough gravel. "I wouldn't do this if I was married." He turned her in his arms and took her mouth in a rough, demanding kiss.

He took a step forward, and she took one backwards until she was pressed between the hard, cold concrete wall of the building and the hard, hot concrete wall of his chest. Good thing he held her tightly, otherwise, she was likely to slide down the wall to the floor. He moved his hands to her ass and jerked her up against his stiff cock. Without conscious thought, she jutted her pelvis against his.

He pulled his mouth away with a groan.

"You have to give me a moment. I'd rather not point the way, if you get my drift."

She smiled. "Lucky women. We can hide our arousal."

"Sometimes," he said. "But right now? I can smell yours."

She swallowed hard. "You can?"

"Oh yeah. Like the sweetest nectar. And your eyes."

"What about my eyes?"

"Honey, every emotion shows on your face. Your eyes are big and dilated. Your lips... Oh my God, your lips are swollen and red and—" He released her and took one step back. "That isn't helping."

She couldn't help it. She grinned. She'd known most of the men in this part of Texas all her life. She liked them all just fine. But none of them affected her like this Yankee did, and she was mighty pleased she wasn't alone in this... whatever this was.

Five

It took a good twenty minutes to collect Marti's purse and say all their goodbyes before they finally headed to Eli's SUV. By the time they exited the hotel, a light rain had just begun to fall. They raced for the parking lot, laughing as Marti tried to run in her three-inch heels.

As soon as her door closed, Marti slipped off her shoes with a sigh and leaned the passenger seat back.

"My puppies are howling," she said.

"I do not understand how women can wear those high-heel shoes. They look like torture."

"And they feel like torture, too." She leaned over the console between them. "I call them high hells."

The front of her dress shifted, and the neckline gaped, exposing the black lace of her bra. He bit back a groan and adjusted slightly in his seat. "That's sounds about right. I can promise you a good foot rub later if that helps."

She leaned against the back of her seat with a low moan. "Are you kidding? Drive faster."

He pulled from the parking lot, his wipers swishing

the rain drops away. He rested his arm on her seat back. "I had fun tonight."

"Me, too."

"I usually avoid these things like the plague, but you made tonight bearable."

Laughing, she said, "Bearable?" She slapped both hands to her chest. "Be still my racing heart. I don't know if I can take many more compliments this evening."

He reached over and took her hand. "You know what I mean." He kissed her palm. Her hand quivered in his fingers, which made him smile. Nice to know that she was as affected by him as he was by her.

"Eli," she said softy, "tell me about your wife."

The SUV kept traveling forward, but that was about all that moved. Eli froze, took a deep breath, and then squeezed her hand before letting it go.

"My marriage. Well, long story short. I met Gina in eleventh grade. We went steady off and on throughout high school. Ended up going to different colleges. After the first semester apart, she transferred to Columbia where I was doing my undergrad work. We married in our sophomore year, way too young, let me add. My parents, who are saints, kept us both in college. Gina doubled up on classes and graduated in three years as a teacher. She worked while I was in medical school." He drew a deep breath before continuing. "On Match Day—do you know what that is?"

Marti shook her head.

Eli cleared his throat. "During the senior year of med school, students interview with various residency programs, trying to get a hospital to offer them a post-graduation slot. We fill out a form, ranking what specialty we want, the residency programs we want, and so forth. The various hospitals and residency programs do the same. Then a computer program eats all that data and spits out who is going where for their residency. Match Day is always the third Friday of March and the wait is nerve-wracking. Not everyone gets matched and a resident offer. Some doctors get more than one offer. But everyone finds out that day. I was fortunate that I matched at Johns Hopkins. It was my number one choice."

He paused, staring straight ahead at the shiny black road. Heavier rain fell, plopping loudly on the SUV's metal roof and hood. The wipers were at medium speed and just barely able to keep up with the volume of water. His tires splashed through puddles, throwing up water alongside the doors.

Marti kept quiet. He knew she was waiting for him to go on, but this next part was hard to tell. He felt so much at fault.

Finally, he sighed and plunged forward, hoping his voice wouldn't crack. "So, Gina planned a party, a celebration for my match. She invited both families and all our friends. We were on top of the world. At the last minute, she decided she needed a few more bottles of champagne. I told her we had plenty, but she was determined that this party would be a major success. She stopped on the way home from work to grab the bottles and..." He bit his lip before continuing. "It's so crazy. It was a small store we'd been to a million times. Really nice older couple. She got her champagne and headed toward checkout when some kids decided that night was the perfect night to rob the place."

"Oh dear Lord, Eli," Marti whispered.

He shook his head, not wanting to stop until he was finished. "One of the kids was in her class. He saw her and called her by name. The other kid said something about leaving no witnesses and shot Gina. Just shot her. A bullet through the heart. And she was gone."

Marti grabbed his hand and held on. "I don't need to know more. That's enough."

He glanced over and then back to the road. "Let me finish, okay?"

"Okay, but only if you want to," she said, her voice thick.

"The kid from her class freaks and runs out. The other kids get nervous, and then they run too. The owners weren't hurt. The kid from her class told his parents, who turned in the whole group. So many lives ruined that night."

The car was silent except for the swish of the wipers and the splash of tires rolling over wet pavement.

"Holy hell, Eli. I don't know what to say."

He shrugged. "There's really nothing to say. It's been seven years, and life does continue even when you don't think you'll live through the pain."

"I don't know how you survived."

"One day at a time. Literally, I took it one day at a time. I got up, did what I had to do, and went to sleep. The next day, I did the same. I had my work. I did Doctors Without Borders and ended up in Afghanistan. That'll make you appreciate living."

"I'm just stunned. And so impressed."

"Don't be. I think the first time I went overseas at the end of my residency, I went hoping I would die. I'd be remembered as a brave doctor doing noble work." His chuckle lacked any humor. "Instead, I found hundreds, no thousands, of people who were much worse off than I was. Losing my wife was tragic, but these people had also lost spouses, along with children and parents and homes.

It helped me keep my perspective about life. I came home ready to do as much good as I could for my patients."

He pulled the SUV to a stop a couple of feet from the steps that led up to her porch. "Talking about my wife is a great date killer, isn't it?" He smiled.

"Hey, I'm the one who pushed. Come on in. We'll have coffee, and I'll tell you all about the time in high school where I took a dare to run my panties up the flagpole."

This time, when he chuckled, the sound was light and full of amusement. "That's a story I want to hear. I have an umbrella in the rear seat if you want to wait for me to come around for you."

"Heck no. I'm not going to melt. I say it's a mad dash for the porch and every man, or woman, for himself. Ready? One, two, three, go." On go, she flung open her door, jumped out and ran. He did the same from his side.

She splashed through the puddles, her laughter making his heart swell. Her feet made slapping sounds as she bounded up her steps to the porch. He followed, loving the sound of her voice as it echoed off the porch ceiling.

"I love the rain," she said. "Love it, love it, love it. Nothing like huddling under blankets and listening to the pounding of rain on the roof." She swung around to face him. "Don't you?"

Her smile pulled him like a magnet. Catching her around her waist, he pressed her against her door and swept his mouth over hers. Her lips were cold and wet from the rain, but when she parted them, his tongue was welcomed into her warm mouth. She moaned and pulled him tight, wrapping one leg around his calf. He pulled his mouth away long enough to change his angle, take a breath, and recapture hers in a deeper kiss that sent his insides spinning like a tornado.

"Let's go inside," she said, leaving a chain of kisses across his cheek and up his neck. "Get out of these wet clothes. Maybe find some towels."

Before he could reply, the sound of an ATV broke through the rain, and a voice from the yard called, "Marti."

Her leg dropped to the floor. She straightened and slid from under him. "Yeah. Pedro? Is that you?" Marti walked to the edge of the porch. "What's wrong?"

"Princess Diana is in labor. Grisham says her foaling started about six or so but he said you'd want to know."

"Thanks. I'll change clothes and be right down."

Pedro turned to leave, and then added, "And Calico's delivering, too."

Marti laughed. "It's her third time. She's an old hand."

Pedro waved and zoomed back toward the barn.

"Sorry, Eli, but I've got to cut tonight short." She leaned forward and kissed him, open-mouthed, hot and hungry. "And just when it was getting good," she said, followed by a long sigh.

She unlocked her door and stepped through, Eli following as though pulled by an invisible string.

When she noticed him behind her she said, "Great." Holding up both hands, shoes dangling off her fingers on the left and the right holding her purse, she added, "My hands are full. Can you unzip me? I need to change." She turned her back to him.

"Sure." Feeling a little dazed, he reached for the six-inch zipper that started in the small of her back and cupped her heart-shaped ass to end just below. As he glided the slider down and the zipper teeth separated, the strings of a teeny black thong were exposed. Blood raced below his waist as his cock filled and strained against his zipper. He groaned. "You're killing me."

Laughing, she hurried toward the staircase, climbing it two steps at a time. Her dress fell off her shoulders as she reached the top. She looked over her shoulder and winked. "Another night, maybe?"

"Another night, definitely," he called up the stairs as she disappeared from view.

He shook his head while uttering, "Damn," under his breath. Marti was so different from other women he'd dated in his life. She was like twirling a lit firecracker between your fingers. You kind of knew it was going to hurt when it exploded, but playing with it made your heart race with excitement.

Heavy boots on the wooden steps had him refocusing to the present. Marti raced down the stairs, pausing to jump from the third one over the last two and landing with a loud thud. She was still tugging down her shirt when she landed.

"Hey! You're still here." She grabbed his face and pulled him in for a kiss. "That's all I've got time for," she said with a chuckle.

He followed her into the kitchen. "What can I do to help?"

She lifted a rain slicker off a peg. "Nothing. We have to let nature take its course." He opened his mouth to reply, but she added, "Yes, yes, I know. You're a doctor. Sorry, Dr. Eli. You're the wrong kind."

He rolled his eyes with a laugh.

The rain, which had been steady, was now pounding the roof in sheets. Lightning lit up the kitchen, followed by a flickering of the lights. A boom of thunder shook the walls.

"Is God usually this mad at Texas?" Eli asked.

Marti howled. "No kidding. Nah. God loves Texas, haven't you heard? We need this rain so bad that nobody's going to complain." She tossed the slicker over her head. "Want to hang around and watch a foal come into the world?"

The idea intrigued and terrified him. Horses. No. But a baby horse? He could handle that.

"Yeah, I think I do."

She tossed him the other slicker hanging on the wall. "Use Dad's slicker. You're already wet, but we'll get drenched as soon as we step outside." She eyed him and said, "I don't think your shoe size is the same as his. Dad has huge feet, but if you want to wear his boots, you might be able to save those fancy shoes of yours."

Eli looked down at his two-thousand dollar Brooks Brothers loafers. "These might be beyond saving."

"Hope they weren't expensive."

He shrugged. "Not too bad." He smiled. "Totally worth tonight's date."

"Aww. Aren't you sweet? Want the boots?"

"Don't worry about it. I do have another pair of shoes in the car."

"Super. Let's head out." She grabbed his hand as she walked past. "I would suggest we walk down, but not tonight. We're taking your SUV."

Once back in his vehicle, she said, "U-turn and go back toward the road. There's a gravel path to the barn." As he did as she instructed, she said, "Sorry about all the water we're getting in your car."

"It's leather. It'll survive."

He was more worried about surviving Marti than his seats surviving a little water.

Following in her instructions, he found the red barn, which was barely visible through the heavy downpour.

"Park over there," she said, pointing beside an older model green truck. "Grisham will be leaving, and I don't want to block him in."

When the car stopped, she flung herself out and raced through the open barn door. He turned off the engine and reached behind his seat. One of his habits held over from residency was keeping a packed duffle in his backseat. Often he'd found himself needing a fresh set of scrubs because of blood or some other bodily fluid. Duffle bag in hand, he ran through the rain and into the barn, stopping short when he entered.

Marti stood at the far end with a young man. A middle-age man leaned on a stall door. Between Eli and the others were numerous stalls. Horses who obviously knew he didn't like them glared from all of them. Yeah, he'd had this nightmare before, but this time, he wasn't going to wake up.

The main corridor was swept clean. The odor was mostly fresh straw lightly scented by horse flesh. The hallway lights were on at his end but off at the far end.

He straightened and took a step. The horse to his right whinnied. He didn't turn his head, but marched forward toward the threesome. As he neared, Marti said, "No, no. I'll be fine. You go on home, Grisham, and be with your family. It's after midnight. Tomorrow will come early enough. And you too, Pedro. Get some sleep. If I need help, I'll call. I promise. Princess Diana would probably rather we all go away and let her do her job in peace."

The older man—Grisham, he assumed—removed his hat and scratched his head. "You're the boss, but seriously, call me if there's any problem at all. In fact, call Dr. Grayson first and then call me."

Marti smiled and patted the man on the shoulder. "Georgie Grayson'll be my first call in the morning. I promise. Now, get home. Both of you."

Both men left, grumbling to each other as they did.

"Now you," she said to Eli.

"Me? What about me?"

"You need to get out of those wet clothes and shoes."

He arched an eyebrow. "I'm not sure I know you well enough for a free strip show."

She laughed and patted her jeans pocket. "I might have some one dollar bills around here."

He snorted.

"Seriously," she continued. "There should be some newspaper in the office to stuff into those shoes. Might help soak out the water."

He saluted, well aware that there wasn't enough newspaper in the world to save his shoes. "Will do. Now, where's the office?"

The office was a small, dusty room with a desk, chair, and phone on the wall. It didn't appear as though it was used for much, but he suspected that back when this old barn was built, this room had seen a lot of action. He did as instructed, stuffing his now-ruined shoes, and changed into jeans and a polo he had in the bag. Truthfully, the dry briefs were the most welcome change. Something about cold, wet undies made a man shrivel up.

Marti snatched his wet clothes from his arms when he walked out. "I'll just hang these up to dry."

That was fine, but he'd pretty much written off his tux along with his shoes.

"Ready to meet Princess Diana?" Marti asked.

"Sure." *Not really.* His heart shivered at the thought of getting near a full-grown horse, even one who'd be preoccupied with labor. Embarrassingly, his fingers twitched with a slight nervous shake.

After draping his wet tux over railings, she led him to the last stall, which was at least double the size of the rest. The upper portion of a Dutch door was open, providing a clear view of a white horse resting on her side, her breaths coming in pants and snorts.

"You sure she's in labor? I mean, shouldn't she be grunting or something?"

Marti snorted. "You've seen too many human drama queens deliver. Horses are pretty calm. Come on. We'll go in."

He took an involuntary step back. "No, that's okay. I wouldn't want to bother her."

She looked at him, then at the horse, and nodded. "Fine. I'm going in to check on her. I'll be back."

He stood in the open doorway and watched as Marti calmly approached the horse and squatted, resting her butt on her heels.

"Hey girl," she said quietly as she stroked the horse's neck. "You're doin' great. Really great. I can't wait to meet your baby. What a good mother you're going to be."

The horse's breathing slowed. Marti's quiet reassurances seem to help calm the laboring mare. Princess Diana blew out a snort and lifted her head. Marti continued cooing and stroking. Finally, the mare settled into the straw. Marti rose and walked back to Eli.

"I'd like to leave the door open so I can make sure she's okay. This is her first one, and I want her to remain calm. Grab a couple of hay bales, and we can sit." She gestured toward a stack of square bales across the aisle in another empty stall.

"Sure." He went over, grabbed the first bale, and reeled backwards.

"Careful," she warned. "Those might be a little heavy. Hold on, I'll come help."

"No, no," he grunted out. "I've got it."

He staggered back to Princess Diana's stall and dropped the bale to the floor. He saw Marti grin.

"You did that on purpose," he said, squinting his eyes as though he was mad.

She laughed. "You did great. That one probably weighs about seventy-five pounds. There are some smaller ones in there that weigh closer to fifty."

He flexed his biceps. "Impressed, huh?"

Marti shook her head with an amused smile. "Oh yeah. Wet panties and everything."

He chuckled, but the mention of her panties, especially wet panties, aroused him. He turned away before she could see the effect her casual comment had on him. No use embarrassing himself like a teenage boy.

Going back to the stall, he grabbed a second, albeit smaller, bale and added it to the first. "There. That should hold us."

After a quick glance at her horse, Marti adjusted one bale so that she was seated in direct sight of her horse.

"Now," she said. "What's the mystery favor you keep hinting about?"

Six

Eli dropped onto the hay bale. “Yeah. The favor.” He sighed. “I have this patient. For his privacy, I won’t tell you his name, but he’s a teen. A great kid. Lost his legs in a horrific accident.”

“Oh,” Marti said. “You must mean Joe Manson. Poor kid.”

“You know Joe?”

“Everybody around here knows Joe. He was on the fast track to the Olympics. Really popular kid. Worked here with the horses a couple of summers back. He could ride like the wind. Took to it like he’d been riding all his life. He’s your patient, huh?”

“Let’s just say, I have a teenage double amputee male.”

“Fine. Joe’s a common name. Could be anybody.”

He explained about Joe and the challenge of getting this depressed teenager out of a wheelchair. He finished with his confession of having a fear of horses.

Marti walked over to the laboring horse and ran the palm of her hand along the mare’s protruding side. “You told a little white lie to get Joe going. No one would condemn you for that."

"Yeah, well, it's not exactly a lie." His balls shriveled up at the confession. He waited for her to laugh, which would only further add to his humiliation.

She whipped her head toward him and nodded. "Okay. I can understand that. They're big, and if you've not been around them, they can be intimidating."

Her calm acceptance caught him off guard. "Ridiculous, right?"

She rose and came back to sit by him. "You're not the first guy I've dated who was antsy around horses. You should see some of the teen offenders I get. The first time a horse snorts at them, they freak, but they get over it. Have you ever been on a horse?"

"My history with horses isn't great. I was kind of an awkward kid. Overweight. Glasses. A summer camp from hell. You get the picture."

"You're not geeky now." Rocking over, she bumped his shoulder with hers. "Fact is, you're kind of hunky."

Heat flared to his face.

She laughed. "Now I've embarrassed you."

He grinned. "Maybe a little."

"So what's the favor?"

His responding sigh was a long, loud exhale. "Joe challenged me to learn to ride a horse while he learns to walk on his new legs, with both of us showing our progress at the end of the summer."

Snapping her fingers, she said, "No problem. Heck, I can have you roping cattle by then."

He grimaced. "I'll be happy with just staying on the horse."

"Been bucked off?"

"Couple of times. You?"

She nodded. “Oh, yeah. Been there, done that. That’ll leave some sour memories, not to mention a sore butt.”

“I—” He pointed into the stall. “We have action.”

Marti was so involved just looking at the sharp angles and strong chin of this incredible man that she’d completely lost focus on why they were sitting in a barn in the middle of the night. She swiveled her head toward Princess in time to see a large gush of fluid pouring forth.

“There goes the bag,” she said, her hands twitching nervously. “It’s so hard to just sit here and let her do the work. I want to help.” She looked at Eli. “Ever seen a horse delivery?”

“Nope. Tons of human babies but no horses.”

“Well, our job is to do nothing, unless she gets into distress. I’ve attended a number of foalings, and I always want to do something.”

He smiled. “Hard to just sit. You seem like the type of woman who likes to take charge, and likely, you get it right most of the time.”

Her heart exploded in her chest with pride. No doubt she was preening like a peacock. She knocked shoulders with him again. “You say the nicest things.”

“How long?” he asked, tilting his head toward the laboring horse.

“Hard to say. An hour, maybe longer, maybe shorter.”

For the next forty-five minutes, they just sat, watched, and whispered encouraging words to Princess. Poor Princess. She grunted and pushed. Her legs extended straight out as she dealt with the contractions. A foot and then a second foot appeared twenty minutes into the process. A couple of minutes later, a light-colored head came through.

"Will the foal be white too?" Eli asked.

"Princess isn't really white. She's a light gray. The sire is also gray, albeit a little darker than Princess. I expect the foal will be a gray."

"Do you know if it's male or female?"

She shook her head. "Nope. Don't care. I just want healthy."

He nodded. "Got it."

Once the shoulders passed, Princess took a break from pushing, and rested.

"Should we help?" Eli asked. "I mean, usually a human baby pops out at this point."

"Nervous?" she asked with a grin. "Nope. This is totally normal. Mom and baby are resting. They should get going again."

As she'd predicted, ten minutes later, Princess began pushing again, and a foal dropped into the straw. Princess went immediately to work cleaning the baby.

"What about the cord?" Eli asked.

"We do nothing unless we absolutely have too. The cord should slow or stop passing blood to the foal in a few minutes, and then mom will take care of things."

"How can you be so calm? Now I'm itching to do something."

She laughed. "Just like a man—especially a doctor. Sit on your hands. No, wait. I've got a better idea." She took both his hands. "I'll hold them. Will that work?"

He squeezed her fingers, but the caress squeezed her heart at the same time. "That'll work great."

She had no idea who she was tonight. She was never this chatty with a guy, at least not until they'd been on a few dates. But Eli felt right. She hated that her hands were work-roughened. He could notice, could be put off by that. Crap. Now that she thought about it, his hands were softer and less calloused than hers.

He probably dated townies, girls with soft hands and long flowing hair. Sure, she had long auburn hair, but most of the time it was slicked back out of the way. Even that dress she wore tonight gave the wrong impression of who she really was. Oh, she'd loved the sparkle in his eyes when he first saw her. The smile that lit up his face when she'd twirled for him. And then...then when he'd stroked his fingers along the flesh of her back, she'd almost melted. Her knees sure had.

However, tonight's dress wasn't her. Neither were the three-inch heels. She was a jeans, shirt, and boots kind of gal, all of it usually dirty at the end of the day.

Eli stroked his thumb back and forth across her knuckles. Holy Hannah. She almost swayed with lust. The way he kissed and touched her set off bombs that shot electrical voltage from her brain to her toes, with lots of energy rushing directly to every female cell. She wasn't looking for anything, or anyone, long term, although if she were, she might not mind a daily dose of how he made her tingle.

Too bad he was only here for a short time.

But on second thought, maybe it wasn't too bad that he was a short-timer. Hadn't she been saying she wasn't looking for long term? A couple of months of serious tingles would be fun. Possibly a little more than tingles for a couple of months would be fun, too.

While she'd been daydreaming—or would that be early-in-the-morning dreaming?—Princess and her new baby had found their footing and stood. A foal's wobbly legs never failed to charm her, and tonight was no different.

"Want to meet her?" she asked. Now that the foal was here, she could see the ranch had another female on its hands.

"I do." His voice held a tinge of surprise, as though he couldn't believe he wanted to.

Regretfully, she dropped one of his hands, and they eased toward the pair. The foal was grey, as she'd expected. She had a darker patch of grey down her nose. Eli inched his hand toward the foal. His first stroke was slow, only lightly touching the newborn.

He looked at Marti with a broad smile. "Incredible."

"I know."

"Have you picked out a name for this little one?"

"I haven't," Marti said. "Got a suggestion?"

"Duchess."

"Oh. I like that. She'll be Duchess of Boone."

The smile she'd thought was wide stretched farther, and his eyes lit up. "You don't have to do that."

"I want to. It'll make me always remember tonight." Like she could ever forget.

He put an arm around her and hugged. "Thank you. I'm touched."

She startled and snapped her fingers. "Shoot. I forgot about Callie." When he frowned, she added, "The barn cat. She was having kittens, and I totally forgot."

He looked around. "Where is she?"

"Office, if she follows her normal pattern." They walked out of the stall toward the open office door. "This is her third, and last, set. She's got an appointment with Dr. Georgie Grayson. Our veterinarian," she explained when he looked confused.

"I didn't see her when I changed clothes earlier."

"Ah, but did you climb under the desk?"

He chuckled. "Can't say that I did."

She lifted the chair away from the desk and climbed under. "Hey there, Momma." She pulled a wooden box lined with soft towels from under the desk. Inside, Callie rested with six kittens nursing away. "Good job, Callie." She stoked the cat. "Looks like some fine mousers you've got there."

"Do all barns have cats?"

Chuckling, Marti said, "I don't know. We always have. They're invaluable for keeping the pests under control."

"You'll keep all these kittens?"

"Doubtful. Most will go to homes where their main job is loving humans. We'll probably keep a couple. But I've got a month or so to decide on that." She lightly stroked a finger along one of he kittens. "Isn't she beautiful?"

"You can tell boys from girls this early?"

She laughed. "Nope. I'm right about fifty percent of the time."

Callie's birthing box had been layered with towels and blankets. Marti removed the bloodiest one from the birth, leaving Callie and her kittens resting on a clean towel.

With both births over, the evening's adrenaline surge sagged. A weariness draped over her like a wet blanket, but she wasn't ready to leave Princess and Duchess. The more she thought about the name Duchess, the more she really loved it. So perfect.

"I'm having an energy slump," she confessed.

"You ready to go?"

"Oh, no. I want to watch Princess and Duchess for a while, make sure everything is okay. But you don't have to stay. Really."

"You trying to get rid of me?" he asked with a wink.

"Nope. Just giving you permission to head out. I'm used to early mornings or late nights."

"Me too." He put an arm around her. "Let's find our bales and watch for a while. Sound good?"

They settled back on the hay, his arm snuggly about her shoulders. She leaned against him. It'd been a long time since she'd done that, rested against a man's chest. His warmth heated the side of her head. A strong, slow heartbeat lulled her eyes closed. Just for a moment, she told herself.

"How long she been asleep?" She recognized Grisham's voice.

"Maybe an hour or so," Eli said. "It was a long night."

"She's awake," Marti said, struggling to separate herself from Eli's comfortable chest. He shook his arm, and she chuckled. "Dead?"

"Maybe a little."

"What time is it?"

"A little after five," Grisham said. He leaned on the open stall door's frame. "She's a beauty."

Marti smiled and pushed her hair out of her eyes. "I know."

"Thought of a name?"

"Duchess," she said. "Duchess of Boone."

"We didn't get a chance to meet last night," Eli said. "Eli Boone."

The older man held out his hand. "James Grisham."

"Sorry. I should have done that." She yawned.

Eli stood. "I'd better get going."

"How about some coffee? Breakfast maybe?"

He shook his head. "Got a meeting at the hospital later today. I need to go home and change."

"Your tux is still pretty damp," Marti said, fingering the sleeve of the jacket.

Eli pulled his pants, jacket and shirt down from where

they'd been hanging and rolled them into a ball. "No problem. I'll let my cleaners deal with them."

"I'll walk you out," she said.

"Nice to meet you," Eli said to Grisham, who nodded.

Marti took his hand, and they walked to his SUV. The rain had stopped, but there were running streams and mud everywhere.

Eli tossed his damp bundle and emergency duffle into the backseat and slammed the door. "Have to say that this was an interesting date," Eli said.

"Yeah, I don't usually provide a live birth as entertainment."

He pulled her in close and wrapped his arms around her. "Thank you." He kissed her, his lips full and warm on hers. "I had a wonderful time."

Wrapping her arms around his waist, she snuggled against him. "I did, too."

She pressed her mouth to his, sliding her tongue through his parted lips. His tongue stroked hers, and she moaned. He glided his hands down her back until he cupped her bottom. Then he pulled her against the thick bulge behind his zipper.

She broke the kiss with a long sigh. "I better let you go."

"I know," he said. "Tonight, or maybe I should say last night, was great."

She stepped back and tilted her head. "Where did you learn to dance?"

Surprise flashed in his eyes. "Excuse me?"

"Dancing. You were as smooth as glass. How'd you learn to dance like that?"

He chuckled. "My mother insisted. I had to go to all these country club functions growing up, so she made me take dance lessons."

"Well, they paid off. Maybe we can hit Leo's Bar one night for dancing."

"Maybe we can." He checked his watch, the first time she'd noticed he was wearing one.

She didn't know the brand, but even she could recognize an expensive piece of jewelry.

"I hate to do this, but I've got to go."

She nodded and backed out of reach. "Me, too. Animals to feed. New babies to play with."

"Thanks again. I'll call you...about the riding thing."

"Sure." Her heart sank a little. He'd call about the favor he wanted, but not about another date? Okay, she could admit she was a tad disappointed he didn't immediately ask her out again, but she could play it cool. That's who she was. Cool-as-a-cucumber Marti. "See you later," she said, adding a little wave.

She turned and headed toward the barn, refusing to let her head swivel back toward him. She could be as cool as any guy when it came to dating.

She sighed. He'd obviously seen through the fancy dress and shoes. Her calloused hands had given her real self away.

He was a Harvard-trained physician.

She was a Texas cowgirl.

That combo didn't even sound logical in her mind.

Sort of like if she decided to breed her best bull with a donkey. Doesn't work.

Seven

The week started with a downed fence that ate up Monday. A group of stubborn moms and calves gave her a run for her money, not to mention a splitting headache on Tuesday. By Wednesday, she was ready to call it done. The cattle wouldn't behave. The fences wouldn't stay where they were supposed to. A bull decided to have a day with the ladies by busting through from his field to theirs.

To put a cherry on her crappy-week sundae, Eli didn't call. She'd thought about last Saturday quite a bit and the more she thought about it, the more she'd have bet money she wasn't the only one feeling something during those kisses. She wasn't that out of practice, was she?

If she realistically looked at the situation, it was obvious they were oil and water as a couple. Still, it would have been nice to think he'd been slayed by her sexiness.

She dumped a large horse turd into a bucket. Yeah, that pretty much described her life.

On Thursday, a large truck turned onto the Flying Pig drive and stopped near the barn. Out in the pasture checking on the new calves, Marti noticed the delivery truck but didn't head back. Grisham was there and could handle whatever the situation entailed.

She'd just swung down off Rascal when her phone beeped with a text message.

Grisham: *Can you head back? You need to deal with this delivery.*

Marti groaned with a sigh. She didn't have time for more crap today. She had to tag those new calves. Still, her foreman rarely, if ever, needed help with anything.

Marti: *Heading back. Be there in ten.*

She finished putting an ear tag on a calf, all the while staring down a pissed-off mom. "There," she said to the cow. "Done. He's all yours." She pushed the baby bull toward his momma, who led him away, stopping a couple of times to give death stares. Marti couldn't suppress her chuckle.

Rascal had her back at the barn in under ten minutes. A grinning Grisham stood with a young man in a shirt monogramed with the name of a local trucking company.

"Hi, I'm Marti Jenkins," she said, pulling off her glove and extending her hand. "How can I help you?"

"I have a delivery for Princess Diana and the Duchess of Boone. And another for Callie. Where do you want 'em?"

Marti wrinkled her brow in confusion. "Excuse me?"

"He has a delivery for—" Grisham started.

"I heard what he said. I'm just confused."

The guy shrugged. "Maybe this will explain it." He handed her a long envelope.

Marti ripped it open and read.

Dear Princess Diana,

Congratulations on the Duchess's birth. She's a beauty for sure. Share your treats with dad.

Eli Boone

"You have got to be kidding me," she muttered. "Well, show me whatcha got," she said to the delivery guy.

He opened the back of the truck and, with Grisham's help, unloaded two wooden crates. Once that was done, he nodded, climbed in his truck, and left.

"Get a hammer or something and let's pry these open."

"Got one while I was waitin'," he said. He pulled a couple of nails from the lid and lifted the wooden top. "Goodness." Grisham was grinning like he'd just won a lottery.

Marti shook her head with a chuckle. Inside were carrots, apples, pumpkin, bananas, grapes and a tin of horse peppermints. "What's in the other one?"

A letter lay inside.

Good morning, Callie. Hope all your kittens are nursing well. Enjoy the treats. Eli Boone

In this crate was cat chow and kitten chow, for when the kittens were ready for food other than Callie's milk, and a number of ropes and other climbing toys, sure to keep everyone in the feline family happy.

"I can't believe he did this." She stared at the crates, her mind running a million thoughts at one time. She'd kind of written him off, decided he'd come to the same conclusion as she about the combination of oil and water. This was...well, so unbelievably sweet.

"The man's smitten," Grisham said.

"No, he's not. He's just...thoughtful."

Thoughtful. Yes, that's what he was. His mother had obviously taught him manners.

"Say what you will, but no man is this thoughtful unless he's smitten."

She smiled, Grisham's words meaning more than he knew. "Nah," she said. "He's just bein' a nice guy."

Grisham snorted but, to her relief, changed the subject. "You get all the calves tagged?"

"Nope, but I had an idea. Let's do the tagging when we do the vaccinations. No reason not to, right?"

"Well, we've always tagged before that."

"But do we have to? I mean, Pedro and I spent all morning chasing calves and pissing off mommas. Every momma out there knows which calf is hers."

Grisham shrugged. "Okay. We'll try it your way this year. Your daddy would have a stroke."

Marti laughed. "Let's not mention this to him when he calls, okay? Nothing gained if we don't try new stuff. Be sure that Princess gets some treats, but make sure to spread it out among all the horses. Heavens knows Princess is spoiled enough."

He nodded. "If that isn't the truth. The rest of the horses'll enjoy it."

She walked away wearing what she knew was an overly broad grin. Her parents had left her in charge, but she knew Grisham still had questions about her decision. He felt that, with his years of experience, he should be making decisions about things like tagging the calves. No matter that this was a small victory, she couldn't help but be pleased.

Now, her next major decision was whether to call Eli and thank him or just send a text. The only problem with that plan was she didn't have his cell phone number. He'd always called from the clinic.

Or maybe she should actually write a thank-you note. That's what her mother and her grandmother would have done. She hadn't written a thank-you note since college graduation and wasn't sure she remembered how.

Since it was almost noon and she'd already been pulled from her job, she headed for the house for a quick sandwich. As she neared, she saw a white, insulated box sitting by the front door. Picking up the pace, she hurried on the porch, stopped, and smiled.

Eli had struck again.

In the kitchen, she cut the box's tape and lifted out a cold bottle of 2006 Dom Perignon champagne and a note.

Congratulations on the new filly. She's a beauty. Here's to the Duchess of Boone.

Eli

Her cheeks ached from her wide smile. Now she *had* to call him and thank him. A written note would take too long. Plus, she really needed to call him while she still had the nerve.

The receptionist at Riverside answered, "Riverside Orthopedics. May I help you?"

"Yes. This is Marti Jenkins. I'd like to speak to Dr. Boone, please."

"I'll put you through to his nurse."

Music played through the receiver for a couple of minutes before a female voice said, "This is Debbie."

"Hi, Debbie. This is Marti Jenkins. I'd like to speak with Dr. Boone."

"Can you tell me the problem? If this is a medical call, I'll need to pull your patient record."

Marti felt the flush to her cheeks. "No, no. This is a personal call."

"I'm happy to take a message. Dr. Boone is with patients and doesn't like to be disturbed unless it's an emergency. Is this an emergency?"

Embarrassed beyond words, Marti wanted to hide in her closet. Of course Eli didn't take personal calls while seeing patients. What was she thinking? She wasn't, and that was the problem. He'd probably be upset that she'd even called the office. What doctor wanted all his staff to know his personal business?

"No, no emergency. I'll talk with him later."

"All right."

Marti pushed the end button, dropped her head on the table, and waited for the earth to open and swallow her. That sounded like the best way out of the horrifying situation. Okay, so *horrifying* might be an overstatement, but she felt like a junior high dweeb.

One date and she was calling him at the office? *Argh.* This wasn't her. She should have left him a message at his house.

Of course, she didn't have that number either.

A written thank-you note then. She'd even drive into town to mail it, and it would for sure get to him overnight.

The rest of her afternoon was eaten away with writing the note (at least ten different versions until she got the wording *just* right). She knew she'd lose whatever afternoon was left by driving the almost hour into town and another hour back.

Grisham sent along a long list of needed supplies, so she ended up spending a couple of hours at the feed and grain store, which was soothing to her humiliated soul. There was something about the aroma of hay, animal foods and other unidentified scents that always lifted her mood. She'd already dilly-dallied around the store for over an hour, but how could she not stop and play with the baby chicks and rabbits?

Running into Zack Marshall also helped her attitude. A consummate flirt, he'd insisted on escorting her around the store, all the while telling her how great she looked, which was, of course, a total lie. Her hair was stuffed under a cap, and her jeans were long past needing to be replaced.

But then he brought up last Saturday evening and how fabulous she'd looked at the gala. She started to remind him that he'd been there with her best friend, but this was Zack. He meant nothing by this. Flirting was like breathing to him. Neither took any thought or effort on his part.

By the time she started the drive home, she was feeling much better. So what? She'd called Eli at his office. Big deal. His nurse probably told him that she'd called. No biggie. If he called tonight, she could thank him for his thoughtful gifts. If he didn't, he didn't. It wasn't like she'd be carrying her phone with her all evening just in case.

In her bedroom at close to midnight, she plugged her dying phone into the charger. She hadn't been waiting for him to call. That was for sure. She always carried her phone. But she did go to bed with conflicted emotions. A little disappointed he hadn't called, but also a little relieved. To add to her confusion, she wasn't sure which emotion was more prominent.

Friday morning opened with a loud boom. Windows rattled with the thunder. Marti wiggled down into the covers to listen to the rain slashing against the house. Really, did the horses need clean hay and food today? Luckily, she'd drawn the short straw for those jobs today. Barn duty all day. Pedro and Grisham were scheduled to rewire the lower pasture. In this rain, that would be impossible, not that Grisham would admit it. She needed to be at the barn first to rework today's jobs.

Chuckling, she tossed the bedcovers off and staggered to the bathroom to wash her face and brush her teeth. She might have horse duty today, but she didn't have to have the same breath as one.

Grisham beat her to work by ten minutes, but they'd both come to the same conclusion. They wouldn't send any hands out into the fields today unless the job was absolutely necessary. Anything that could be put off would be. The cows had plenty of pasture. The horses, too. So, after turning out all the horses, except Princess and Duchess, Marti gave herself a day off, something she hadn't done in months.

Down time isn't something cattle ranchers get often. Marti was accustomed to doing, not sitting. By nine, she'd cleaned the house, done the laundry and was seriously considering polishing her mother's silver pieces.

Instead, she made a hair appointment at Kathy's Kut and Kurl. Horrible name for a beauty shop, but Kathy Branford was an artist when it came to hair. Marti hadn't had a trim in months, and sadly, her hair showed it. After her beauty shop appointment, she'd enjoy lunch with Delene and Tina.

The Lonestar Grill was crowded when Marti arrived. Parking was at a premium, but she lucked into a spot by grabbing it the second another car backed out. As soon as she walked in, Delene stuck two fingers between her lips and whistled to get Marti's attention.

She laughed and headed to a table near the rear.

"Sorry I'm late," Marti said, sliding into the booth. "You know how slow and picky Kathy can be."

"May be a diva, but she does great work. Let me see the back," Tina said.

Marti twisted around on the bench seat.

"Oh, I like," Delene said.

"Agreed," said Tina.

Marti turned back to the table. "I'm starved. What are you having?"

Drinks and salad orders placed, the three women leaned into the table to gossip.

"I've got all afternoon," Marti began. "I want to know what's happening with you two."

"Nothing," said Tina. "Haven't had a date in a month. Chad dumped me for some slutty blonde, and my mother wants to start carrying bridal gowns in the store. That's it. I'm done. Who's next?"

"Chad dumped you?" Delene asked. "I just saw you with him two days ago."

Marti decided now would be a great time to drink some water and not mention that Chad had asked her out. Seeing how distressed Tina looked, she was glad she'd turned him down. She really hadn't realized there was much between them.

Tina shrugged. "Two days ago? Oh yeah. I was returning his mother's glass cooking dish he'd left at my house."

"Sorry to hear about that," Marti said. "I guess I missed that you two were that involved."

Tina sighed. "We weren't. Not really. I'm just having a pity party for myself." She sighed again. "Why can't we get some new guys in town?"

"We do have at least one," Delene said. "Dr. Hottie." She pointed her finger at Marti. "Now tell all. I want to hear all about him. What a hunk."

"I've heard about Dr. Boone," Tina said. "I ordered new scrubs for a number of the nurses at the hospital, and they came last week to pick up their orders. All of them were blah blah blahing about this guy. What's the story?"

"He's cute. He's nice. He's a great kisser," Marti said.

"And don't look now, but he's walking in the door," Delene said. "With some hot-looking chick," she added.

Marti turned toward the door.

"I said don't look," Delene hissed.

Marti rotated back to the table. "Fine. What's he doing? Did he see me?"

"He's, um, headed this way."

Marti straightened her shoulders and licked her lips, ready for battle.

"Marti?" Eli's deep voice flipped her gut over.

Marti twisted her head until she could look up. "Oh, hi, Eli. Fancy meeting you here."

He chuckled. "I could say the same. Got away from the ranch on a Friday?"

Marti gestured toward the door. "Pouring rain. Pedro and Grisham have everything under control.".

"I'm Eli Boone," he said, holding out his hand to Tina.

"Oh, I'm sorry," Marti jumped in. "Tina. Eli Boone. He's filling in for Hank Kelly. Eli, this is my friend Tina Baker, and you remember Delene Younger from last Saturday."

"Of course. Nice to see you again, Delene. Nice to meet you, Tina. This is Debbie Watts, my office nurse. Debbie, this is Marti, Delene, and Tina."

"Nice to meet you all," she said. "Hope you have a nice lunch." She placed her hand on Eli's forearm, staking her claim, in Marti's opinion. "Eli, I believe the hostess is waiting on us."

He looked toward a table where the hostess stood. "Right, right. You go ahead. I'll be there in a minute. I need to chat with Marti for a sec."

Debbie smiled, and if looks could kill, Marti would be six feet under. "Do you want me to order you a drink while I wait?"

"Tea is fine."

She walked away, her hips swinging like a bell being tolled.

"How's Princess and Duchess?" Eli asked.

"Doing great. Thank you for the surprises. Everyone enjoyed them. Callie's using the rope to escape her babies."

Eli laughed. "Don't blame her at all. Sextuplets can be a handful."

Marti grinned. "I hope you got my note. It was really thoughtful of you to send all the treats."

"And the champagne? Did you enjoy it?"

"Saving it," she said. "Never know..."

He nodded and glanced toward Debbie, who was shooting eye daggers at the three women. "I'd better run. Debbie and I only have an hour for lunch." His eyebrows rose and fell. "We still on for, um, my favor?"

"Sure. Whenever you're ready and available."

"Better go," he said. "Great seeing you. Bye, ladies."

As he left, Delene leaned over the table to whisper, "What favor? Do we need to have the safe-sex talk with you since your parents are out of town?"

"And who's Duchess? And I want to know about the favor, too. Are you holding out on us? Your bestest friends? I don't have a sex life," Tina whined. "Share yours."

Marti lifted her glass of water to take a sip.

"Now you're just being mean," Delene said, sitting back and crossing her arms. "For that, I'm not going to tell you about the upcoming boot sale. I'll let you pay full price."

Marti laughed. "Wow. Way to bring out the big guns."

Tina waved her fingers. "Let's have it."

Over lunch, Marti told them about Saturday. Princess's labor. Duchess's birth. Her falling asleep. She might have downplayed the kisses a little. Okay, she downplayed them *a lot*. She wasn't ready to spill all, even to her best friends.

She also didn't mention Eli's request to learn to ride. She thought he might not want the whole town to know.

By three, the rain had cleared and the afternoon sun was steaming up the area. Outside was sweltering. Marti traded her jeans, boots, and nice blouse for old shorts, grubby T-shirt, and sandals. Even those weren't cool enough for the afternoon heat. Mother Nature was making up for the morning rain, trying to dry everything out by turning up the temperature.

Marti wiped the sweat off her forehead as she walked toward the barn to check on her girls. The stall was empty. All the stalls were empty.

"Grisham," she hollered. "Where's everybody?"

From a distance, she heard, "Outside watching Duchess."

Exiting the rear door of the barn, she found Grisham and Pedro sitting in chairs with cold drinks in their hands.

"Hard at work?" she drawled.

Grisham looked over his shoulder. "Sure are. Hard workin' at doing nothin'."

She chuckled, grabbed a stool, and dragged it over to where the guys were sitting. "Any calves this morning?"

"Two," Pedro replied. "Both females. Both out, cleaned up, and standing under their moms when I found them. Both look good."

"Great," she said. "Got anything else to drink?"

Grisham pointed his bottle toward an ice cooler. "Help yourself."

She pulled out a diet soft drink, cracked the top, and took a long swallow. "Wow, that tastes good." She rolled the icy bottle on her forehead. "Anything on the schedule for this afternoon?"

"You're the boss," Grisham said. "You got anything?"

"Nope."

"Then I guess there's nothing on the schedule."

"You check on the hay lately?" she asked.

"Yep," Grisham said. "Should be ready to cut toward the end of the month, or early in June. Looks like one of our better yields."

"Great. That'll make Dad happy."

"Speaking of, they called today. Wanted to know if they needed to be back for the hay harvest."

Acid splashed up the sides of her stomach. Her parents had checked up on her?

"Oh? What'd you tell them?"

"I said no. You were whipping us all into shape, and we'd be fine without them."

She laughed. "Whipping you into shape? Ha. That'll be the day. Seriously, were they worried about things here? I wonder why they didn't call me."

"Did. Said you didn't answer."

She pulled out her cell and saw that she'd missed two calls and had two voice messages. One from her parents and one from Riverside Ortho. She'd listen to them later.

"You're right. I must have turned the ringer off and forgot to turn it back on."

"Somebody's coming down the drive," Pedro said. "Can't be my date. She's not pickin' me up 'til six."

Marti looked at the teen. "Your date is picking you up and not the other way around?"

Pedro grinned. "What can I say? She insisted. I'm irresistible."

"She probably saw the inside of your truck," Grisham

offered. “No sane person would want to ride in that trash-filled bucket.”

“Hey man, don’t knock my ride,” said Pedro.

“The truth hurts,” Marti said, laughing as she stood. “I’ll see who’s here. Probably a package.”

It wasn’t a package.

Eight

Delene Younger was pounding on Marti's door by the time she got to the house from the barn.

"You know, you could just check to see if it's locked rather than trying to knock it down."

Delene whirled around and slapped her hand to her chest. "Girl! You almost gave me a heart attack."

"What are you doing here? We just saw each other a couple of hours ago."

Delene jabbed her finger toward Marti. "You might fool Tina with that *I fell asleep on him and nothing happened* story, but not me. I know you better than that. And, if that was the honest truth, you wouldn't have picked at your salad and hardly reacted when I said I thought I might shave my head for summer. Then, as soon as you could, you practically ran out of the restaurant. Something happened with Dr. Hottie."

Marti sighed and opened the unlocked front door. "Come on in. Want something to drink?"

Delene followed Marti to the kitchen.

"Got a Diet Coke?"

Marti lifted an eyebrow. "Need you ask?"

She opened the refrigerator and pulled out a couple of Diet Cokes and joined Delene at the kitchen table.

"So," Delene said as she popped the tab on the can. "What happened?"

"Everything I told you was true. I swear."

"Uh-huh. But you didn't tell us everything."

"Need a glass for your Coke?"

Delene snorted. "You really don't want to say, do you?" Then she gasped. "You didn't sleep with him, did you? On a first date? That is so not like you."

"Right. We had a great toss in the hay after watching Princess give birth. Nothing sexier than amniotic fluid, a wet, slightly smelling newborn, and watching a new mother lick the afterbirth. I mean, who wouldn't want to strip and screw after that?"

Delene's loud, deep laugh echoed around the kitchen. "You do have a point."

Marti smiled and gave in. Delene wasn't just one of her best friends. They'd been together since first grade. "Fine. He kissed me."

Delene shrugged. "I know. You told us that at lunch today."

"I might not have been completely honest at lunch."

Delene leaned forward. "Really? So there *was* kissing going on when I saw you two cuddled on the patio."

"Not there, well, there too, but mostly when we got to my house. The first kiss was sweet. Soft. Really, just barely a kiss. But then...*ohmigod*, he backed me into my door and kissed me like a starving man finding a loaf of bread. It wiped my mind of any thoughts but how to get closer to him." She looked at Delene. "And the only way we could have been closer would've been skin to skin. It was like my soul wanted to climb inside him. It was the most erotic, sensual kiss I've ever had."

"Better than the ex?"

"Ha. No comparison. If he hadn't been holding me against my door with his body, I probably would've melted in a puddle of begging lust. I swear. I was thinking about inviting him in—and yes, I know I've never gone to bed with a guy on the first date—when Pedro rode up and told me Princess was in labor. Of course, I had to go."

"Of course. I mean,"—Delene held up her hands like the scales of justice—"on this side we have a horse going through a totally natural process," she raised one hand higher, "and on this hand, we have a hot, sexy doctor that you're having lusty-pants for." She raised the other hand. "Who wouldn't have chosen the bloody, smelly horse over the great-smelling, handsome man?"

Marti laughed. "Well, when you put it that way..."

Delene shook her head. "Anyway, choice made. Smelly horse won. So you had a lusty-pants moment."

Marti gave her a sheepish look. "It kind of wasn't the *only* one."

"Thank the heavens. I thought I was going to have to slap you."

"Maybe I was more into him than he was to me, you know? Guys are like that. I was obviously sending out lusty vibes, and he was getting them."

"I don't know. He's been in town for what? Three months or so? Surely, if he was a hound dog out for the quick shag, we'd all know it. This town's grapevine is too active."

"Maybe."

"Maybe, nothing. Besides, he stayed *all night* with you to watch a horse deliver. If that doesn't say he's interested, nothing does."

Before Marti could reply, her cell phone rang. She looked at Delene. "Riverside Ortho."

"It's him," Delene said. "Answer it."

"Hello?"

"Hi, Marti. It's Eli Boone."

"Hi, Eli. I do remember your last name." He laughed and lust tugged at her gut.

"I guess you do. It was good to see you this afternoon. Sorry we didn't get a chance to talk."

"Well, you did have a date."

Delene slapped her hand over her own mouth as she snorted.

"Date? Oh, you mean Debbie. No, no. That wasn't a date. I just took her out for a quick bite. We had a heavy schedule this morning and this afternoon."

"Does she know that?" Marti could not believe the words coming out of her mouth. *Shut up*, she ordered.

He laughed again. "I assume so. She works for me. Why?"

"Oh, nothing. What can I do for you, Eli?"

"Stop being a bitch," Delene hissed at her. "Be nice. Lusty-pants, remember?"

Marti waved off Delene.

"I know it's late notice. Seems like I say that a lot. Anyway, I thought I was on call for ortho emergencies at the hospital, but I'm not. I wondered if you'd like to have dinner."

"Dinner? Tonight?"

"Say yes," Delene whispered.

"I'm sorry, Eli. I already have plans for tonight."

"You do not," Delene said, almost loud enough for a person in the county to hear.

"Shoot. I knew it was late notice."

"I'm sorry, too, but I have plans with Delene and Tina."

Delene's eyes shot wide, and then she squinted. Before Marti could react, Delene jerked the phone from her hand.

"Eli? Hi. It's Delene. Remember? We met last Saturday and again today." Delene climbed onto her chair to keep the phone away from Marti. "Marti's dryer buzzed so she had to go take the clothes out."

"Give me that phone," Marti demanded. "Right now."

"Uh-huh. Un-huh. We'd love for you to join us tonight."

"Delene. Stop it." Marti jumped, trying to grab the phone.

"No, absolutely not," Delene told Eli. "We always head to Leo's Bar on Friday nights for dancing. You're more than welcome to join us. Real casual. Just look for us." She paused. "What time?" Delene turned in the chair until she faced the stove. "Well, it's about five now, so I'd say we'll be there by seven or so."

"I'm going to kill you," Marti promised.

"Great. We'll see you there. Oh, here's Marti now."

Delene handed the phone to her with a grin. "Here. I kept him company while you were taking clothes out of the dryer."

Marti scowled. "Sorry about that, Eli. Delene can be a little pushy."

"I like her," Eli said. "She sounds like a fun person."

Marti glared at Delene. "Oh, she's fun all right."

"Tonight, then. Do you mind if I join you ladies?"

"And guys," Marti said. "And sure. If you want to come, come on. But don't feel like you have to just because Delene twisted your arm."

He chuckled. "She didn't twist my arm, and it sounds like fun."

"Super," she said through gritted teeth. "See you there."

As soon as she clicked off, she turned on Delene. "I am going to kill you. You seriously overstepped this time."

"Blah, blah, blah," said Delene. "You don't have very long to look presentable. I'd suggest a bath and maybe fluff up your hair a little. Want me to hang around so you can ride over with me?"

"No. I might put you in a tub of water and hold your head under."

Delene laughed. "See you at Leo's," she said with a wave. "I guess I'd better round up the gang for a night out."

It didn't take two hours for Marti to get ready to go. Leo's and a night with the gang did not demand fancying up.

Still, Eli said he was coming.

Oh, God. *Eli was coming.*

How should she act?

Cool as a cucumber? Interested? Hard to get?

She hated dating and—not that she'd admit this to anyone—one of the reasons she'd accepted Theodore's marriage proposal was so that she didn't have to go on any more dates. Deep in her gut, she'd known, or at least suspected, that how she felt about Theo hadn't been love, or at least not the marrying kind of love. His kisses—no man's kisses—had ever rung her bell like Eli's had.

And the more she thought about it, the more she didn't like losing her mind over a guy. Therefore, her theme for this evening would be to play it cool.

The last thing Marti wanted was to project any sort of anxiety about tonight, so continuing with her "Be

Cool" theme, she didn't arrive at Leo's until well after seven-thirty. The lot was full. She expected the inside would be also. Loud country music spilled out of Leo's double doors onto the porch. Any space on the lot not holding a truck, car, or motorcycle held bar patrons. She might have had better luck if she'd ridden Rascal and hitched him to a post. Whispering a few creative dirty phrases, she circled four or five times until she found one lone sliver of pavement where she could leave her car.

She literally pushed and elbowed her way into the bar. Lots of happy—or drunk—people. She wasn't one of them.

Payback was a bitch, and she intended to remind Delene of that fact.

A loud whistle cut through the momentary silence between songs. Delene madly waved both arms over her head.

With a resigned sigh, she made her way across the dance floor to where multiple tables had been shoved together so that the gang of friends could all be together.

"Saved ya a seat," Tina said, pointing to an empty chair beside her. "You owe me. *Bigly*."

Marti scooted past the usual single crowd—Chad, Zack, Michael, Delene, Tina—and a number of couples who'd married within the last year.

And surprise, surprise. Darling Debbie was among their midst, along with a luscious-looking Dr. Hottie.

"You remember Debbie, right?" Tina asked.

"Sure. Hi, Debbie."

"Hope you guys don't mind me joining you all. Being so new to town, when Eli, I mean Dr. Boone, invited me to join the fun, how could I resist?"

"How, indeed?" said Marti.

Damn it. The green-eyed monster awoke and blew fire.

"I know this one will get y'all up on the floor," the DJ shouted through the speakers. "Grab your favorite guy or girl and get on out here."

Rascal Flatts started singing about fast cars and freedom.

Debbie squealed. "My favorite. Come on, Eli. Let's get our move on."

Eli opened his mouth to reply, but Debbie was up and pulling him along. He smiled and followed, but his smile looked a tad forced.

Marti glared at the group. "Okay. Which of you asshats invited Grabby Debbie to sit with us?"

The guys looked confused. Delene and Tina exchanged glances..

"I swear we didn't," Delene said. "Eli was here when she walked in. She zoomed on him like a magnet, and then there she was."

"Who cares?" Zack asked. "We're all friends here, right? Nothing wrong with extending the group a little."

Delene glared at him, and then turned her back. "So, as I was saying, she just parked her butt with us."

"And it's a cute little butt, right, Chad?" Zack asked.

By some miracle, Delene did not coldcock Zack. Instead, she stood and extended a hand to Michael, the lawyer who'd recently joined a law firm in town. "Want to dance, Mike?"

"Um, it's Michael and sure."

"Great." She grabbed his hand and pulled him away.

"Zack, my man," said Chad. "You're playing with fire."

Maybe Marti wouldn't have to plan a good payback for Delene. Tonight might be its own torture.

"So, what'd I miss?" Marti asked. She looked around. "Am I going to get a drink, or will it be impossible?"

"Impossible if you wait for a waitress. Want me to go to the bar for you?"

"Thanks, Chad. That's very sweet. Since I can see how this night is going, get me a bucket of six beers."

"Yes, ma'am." He saluted and left.

The song ended, and despite what appeared to be Debbie trying to talk Eli into the next one, the couple weaved through the dancers and came back to the table. Eli helped Debbie into her seat then walked around the mass of friends until he could take the chair next to Marti.

"Hi," he said.

"Hi, yourself." *Play it cool. Don't melt all over your chair because he spoke to you. You're cool.*

"You saving a dance for me?"

Marti bit her lip and rolled her eyes up, as though deep in thought. "Yeah. I think I can do that, if Debbie doesn't object."

Apparently her green-eyed dragon had taken over her mouth.

Eli smiled, but it wasn't the same lift of lips he'd given Debbie. This time, his full mouth was stretched wide, and his eyes lit. "I want a slow one."

His voice was deep and rattled through her. Her heart picked up the pace from walk to trot. "Really?"

"Really."

She put her hand on his forearm before she replied, and it took the strength of the gods not to look at Debbie. "I think we can do that."

"Can I get you a drink?"

"Chad volunteered but thanks."

He frowned. "That doesn't make me look good, does it?"

"This isn't a date, so you don't have to feel obligated to buy me drinks."

He scooted his chair closer until their thighs met. He draped an arm on the back of her chair and leaned toward her. "I wanted it to be a date," he said into her ear.

Warm breath circled her ear and trailed down her neck. Fingers of heavy lust stirred the smoldering fire inside.

She drew in a breath. He smelled so good. Sandalwood mixed with something spicy. Add in his pheromones and testosterone, and she was a goner. How in the world had she convinced herself she could remain cool in his presence?

"I wasn't sure after seeing you and your nurse at lunch today."

He fingered her curls, tickling her neck. "I'm not interested in my nurse. She's new to town, and I felt sorry for her. There's only one person I'm interested in." His fingernail dragged softly down the side of her throat.

Her heart charged from trot to full-out gallop under his soft touches. She swallowed. "Yeah?"

"Yeah. If you don't know that, then I'm not doing something right."

"Here's your beer," Chad said, setting a bucket of ice with six beers on the table. "That's thirty-five dollars."

Eli straightened.

Marti didn't know if she should chuckle that Chad was holding out his hand for money or groan that his timing sucked so bad.

Eli pulled two twenties from his pocket. "Keep the change."

"Hey, man. Thanks," Chad said.

"You don't have to do that," Marti murmured.

"Do you really want to sit here tonight in this noisy

bar and drink beer?" He leaned in closer. "Or would you rather go somewhere a little quieter with some soft music and an excellent wine list?"

She looked into his chocolate eyes. There was only one answer to that question.

"Wine?"

Marti dropped her purse in a chair and followed Eli across his living room to his kitchen. She took a seat on a stool at the bar separating the kitchen from the open, spacious living room. "Sure."

"Red or white?" He held up two bottles.

"Whichever you'd prefer."

She was in Eli's home and, damn it, she was nervous. Her mind whirled with a million thoughts, too fast and too many to make any sense. Her heart pounded against her chest. Her breaths were rapid, making her lightheaded.

But her lightheadedness could also be related to where she was. She'd followed him in her car from Leo's, not daring to leave her car parked there in the lot. Whispering Springs was like gossip central when it came to relationships, especially about what would probably be a one-night stand.

At least, she hoped that's what they were here for.

Ruby-red liquid sloshed around in a crystal wine glass

as he handed it to her. "A late-harvest Cabernet Sauvignon from California."

The wine was sweeter than she'd expected. "Delicious."

"Come on," he said, holding out a hand. "That hard stool can't be comfortable. And I do want you comfortable."

He led her to the open living room and took a seat on the enormous wrap sofa.

"I can't believe you found something like this to rent," she said, still standing, still looking around.

"I didn't. I bought it."

She whirled to him. "You bought it? But you're only going to be here six months."

"Sit down, Marti. You're making me nervous. You look like you're ready to make a dash for the door."

He'd taken a seat against the sofa arm. She sat on the next section, adjacent but not pressed right up to him. And he was nervous? She didn't buy that for a second.

"Nice wine," she said, taking a sip.

An inane comment because, of course, he would serve a fine wine, but her mind had stopped sending messages to her mouth.

"It is," he agreed. He put his arm on the back of the sofa. "We can talk about the wine or..."

"Or?" Her voice was barely above a whisper.

"Or we could do this." He took her wine glass and set it on the coffee table along with his. Then, he cupped the back of her head and leaned in for a kiss. Her mouth met his. Both were open, their tongues meeting in a tangle of caresses. A moan rattled deep inside him, and Marti's heart skidded sideways.

She turned on the couch until she was facing him and tried to get closer, but her folded legs on the cushion served as a barrier. Leaning forward on her knees, she snaked her arms around his neck, running spread fingers up into his dark curls.

He moved both hands to her waist and hauled her toward him, sliding down the sofa at the same time. He pulled his legs up onto the cushions while she stretched hers out until they were lying flush, chest to chest and groin to groin.

Breaking the kiss, he adjusted his mouth to take the kiss even deeper, something she'd not believed possible. His tongue thrust into her mouth, licked hers, and withdrew, and then began the cycle again. Very much mimicking lovemaking. Electrical volts shot through her from the top of her head to the bottom on her feet. Her toes curled.

He glided his hands up her sides with soft strokes on top of her shirt. Her breasts swelled and ached with a need to be touched. He complied, running a hand across her breasts. She groaned with relief and leaned away enough to give him access. Taking a breast into his hand, he fondled and massaged. Heat shot through her. She pressed her groin against his hard erection, groaning at the lust escalating inside. Her sex grew heavy with arousal.

He growled, jerking his mouth from hers. "You're killing me," he said, his voice as jagged as gravel.

She ground against him again, while she ran the tip of her tongue along the side of his neck, loving the taste of his salty flesh.

"Yeah," she whispered into his ear. "How about this then?"

She scooted her entire body toward the back of the sofa, and then slipped her hand between them until she could reach his pants. She unfastened them and pushed her hand inside until her fingers wrapped around the solid mass of his cock. She squeezed and ran her hand up and down his length.

"Good God," he moaned. "Don't stop." He grabbed her head and yanked her in for a wet, open-mouthed kiss that utilized his lips, tongue, and teeth. He gnawed gently on her lower lip then drove his tongue deep inside her mouth. All the time, he never stopped his hands, stroking, touching, rubbing, and massaging any portion of her body he could reach. He pinched her nipples through her shirt, then latched his mouth onto her breast through the material.

She arched over him, trying to give him full access to anything he wanted, to any part of her body. She felt his fingers at her waist as he grasped the hem of her shirt. She pulled her hand from his pants and helped him pull her shirt over her head. He stared at her breasts, and she was thankful she'd worn the only lace bra she owned.

"Beautiful," he said. He ran a finger along the lacy trim of each cup, producing a shot of lust through her veins. His tongue traced the same path and then dove between the swells of her breasts.

Breath swooshed from her lungs as her stomach clenched.

"Taste as good as they look," he growled.

He unsnapped the bra's front closure and her breasts fell into his hands. "Sweet baby Jesus," he said, then latched his mouth onto one tip while rolling the other nipple between his fingers.

Arousal flooded her panties. She spread her legs until she straddled one of his thighs. She crushed her sex against his thigh muscles, trying to find some relief from the pressure building inside. She rode his leg, grinding and releasing over and over.

"That's it, baby," he growled into her ear. "Ride me. Ride me hard."

He jammed his thigh between her legs, and she rode. Hard. She no longer had a simple arousal. She was consumed with getting to the peak. It was there, just out of her reach. Her head dropped back, her hair flowing down. She cried out in frustration. It was there, but she couldn't grasp it.

The waist of her pants loosened. Eli shoved his hand inside her panties, finding her swollen nub.

"Let go," he said. "I've got you. Let go. Let me watch you come in my hand."

His fingers stroked her clit. His thumb pushed it. He found her mouth and thrust his tongue inside as his fingers continued their relentless stroking and thrusting.

And then she exploded, thrusting her sex against his hand and fingers. Pulling her mouth away, a loud, low groan rose from her depths. She slammed her eyes shut against the flood of feelings swamping her.

"Don't close your eyes," he said. "Look at me." When she didn't, or couldn't response fast enough, he demanded, "Look at me."

She tugged her heavy eyelids up and met his dark chocolate eyes.

"Good God," she said, embarrassed by how easily he'd brought her to orgasm. She hid her face in his shoulder.

He pulled his hand from her pants and cupped her rear. "You know how to make a guy feel wanted."

"I'm so sorry. I never do that."

"Don't be sorry. Anything but sorry." He put two fingers under her chin and lifted her face until they were eye to eye. "That's the sexiest thing that's happened to me in a long time."

She lowered her eyes, sure her face was flaming. "Still...

kind of rude, you know? Come over, grab a glass of wine, then hump my way to an orgasm."

He threw back his head with laughter and hugged her. "Need a cigarette?"

She shook her head. "I think I need more of this." She took his mouth in a kiss that she hoped conveyed what she really wanted. After a minute, he slid from under her, took her hand, and led her to his bedroom.

Message received.

ELI LOVED the feel of Marti's hand in his. It was strong and soft simultaneously, just like the woman herself...a woman he desired with the heat of a thousand suns. Strong. Confident. A woman who knew what she wanted.

God, he hoped she wanted him as much as he wanted her.

Of course, this wasn't the first time he'd had sex since his wife died. He'd followed Hank's advice and avoided entanglement with women living in Whispering Springs, taking his libido to Dallas a couple of times. He'd made sure the women he bedded knew the night was a one-time thing and probably wouldn't be repeated.

And he'd never brought a woman to his house. That was an absolute rule. No women.

Until tonight.

When she'd walked into the bar, he'd wanted to immediately tag her as his. He didn't want other men thinking she was available, and even he realized that was an insane thought. There was just something about her that called to him. Something that tugged deep inside him. The crazy thing was she was nothing like any other woman he'd ever dated.

Typically, he was drawn to quiet, petite women. Usually blondes too. Oh, and blue eyes.

And yet, it was a tall, strong, muscular cowgirl with brown hair and green eyes who'd stormed into his life with her rattlesnakes and baby animals that made him feel alive once more. He'd believed he'd let himself feel, had learned to sense his emotions again after Gina's death.

He'd been wrong. Dead wrong.

"Oh, Eli. This is gorgeous," she said, looking around his bedroom. She ran her hand down one of the tall cherry wood posts of his bed. "I've always had a thing for massive beds."

"Oh yeah? I've always had thoughts about what could be done with those bedposts."

"Actually," she said, looking at him through her lashes. "I have a thing for anything massive."

He swallowed his chuckle, but found it hard to fight the corners of his mouth that wanted to curl up. "Nothing like a little pressure on a guy."

She smiled. "Oh, you have nothing to worry about." She released his hand, slid her pants down her legs, and climbed into the middle of his bed. She let her bra slip down her arms until she could drop it over the edge. "Show me yours, and I'll show you mine."

She'd unfastened his slacks in the living room, and they'd barely made the ride on his hips from there to the bedroom. A kick of his shoes, a light push, and the material fell down his legs and onto the floor, leaving him dressed in boxers, socks and his oxford shirt. Reaching over his shoulder, he pulled the cotton shirt over his head without unbuttoning it. Who cared if he popped buttons off? He had more shirts.

Marti crawled across the mattress to the edge and sat on her heels. "Stop. Come here."

He walked to where she waited and stood. As she studied him and ran her fingers along his pectoral muscles and down the dark hair of his abdomen, he was glad he still worked out. He was a long way from how he'd looked in college, when looking good took priority. His body might have aged, but he knew more about how to please a woman now than he had then.

"You are beautiful," she said, leaning forward to trace the tip of her tongue around his nipple.

He caught her head between the palms of his hands and held her against him, feeling her warm breaths thread through his chest hair. His heart raced and danced. It might have done a cartwheel or two.

Keeping her head on his chest, Marti walked her fingers down his sides until she got to the waistband of his boxers. She wiggled her fingers under the elastic, and he reflexively sucked in his gut. Stretching the elastic, she eased the boxers down over his stone-hard dick. His erection jutted upward and bounced softly off his abdomen.

"Oh, baby, baby," she crooned. She flicked out her tongue and ran the tip over the head of his cock, along the slit, and then sucked the head between her lips.

He hissed out a cuss word. His knees quaked, and he wondered how long he'd be able to stand there under the torture.

"This isn't working," she said. "Come sit here." She patted the bed beside her.

He stripped off his boxers, pausing long enough at the floor to tug off his socks. Then he sat as directed. She slid off the bed and stood in front of him. Taking a knee in each hand, she pushed his thighs apart and knelt between them.

His heart jumped into his throat. He could barely take

in enough breath. Still, he couldn't look away from the gorgeous woman on her knees in front of him.

"You don't have to do this," he said. "I don't expect—"

That was as far as he got before he saw his dick disappearing between her luscious lips and into her hot, wet mouth.

Damn. He almost lost it immediately. He swallowed, or at least tried to swallow, but his mouth was dry.

She wrapped her hands around the base of his cock and squeezed, softly rotating her hands as she slid them up and down in conjunction with her mouth. When he hit her throat, she hummed, the vibrations tapping the end of his dick. Then she sucked as she pulled back, almost releasing him from her lips before taking him deep again.

He fisted the sheets and spread his knees wider. His balls pulled up, ready to spill. "Stop," he said through gritted teeth. "Stop." He grabbed her head and pulled her away. "Another stroke like that and it's all over for me."

"But I was just getting started," she protested, but the twinkle in her eye gave her away.

"Sorry, you hellion. I'm going to need a minute."

Her hands were still holding him, and she squeezed firmly and held. His orgasm receded, and he was able to take a breath.

"Should I continue?" she asked coyly.

He chuckled. "Not if you want to fuck, and baby, I do want to fuck you."

"Oh yeah? Sounds like we are definitely on the same page." She released him and stood.

"Those need to go," he said, indicating the scrap of lace pretending to be underwear.

She wiggled fingers under the thin straps at her hips. "These?"

"If you ever want to see them again, then yeah. Otherwise, I'm going to break those tiny strings to get to you."

She laughed. "Seeing as I bought them just for you, it might be nice to save them."

His mind whirled. She'd bought them for him? "For me? You expected this?"

"Oh, hell no," she said, slowly lowering the material. "But a girl's gotta have hope." She kicked the panties over by the door and climbed into bed.

He flipped her onto her back. "A guy has fantasies about women like you." He took her mouth in a rough, bruising kiss that held nothing back.

She answered with her mouth. Tongues tangled, breaths shared. It was impossible to tell where one set of lips ended and the other began.

She wrapped her long legs around his waist, bringing her wet core into direct contact with his dick. Her moisture coated his flesh.

"I'm sorry. I don't know if I can go slow this first time. I'm afraid it's going to be hard and fast."

"Who told you I didn't like hard and fast?" she murmured. "Well, hard over fast for sure, but hell yes. Move on. I'm dying here."

He pulled a condom from a bedside drawer then sat back on his knees. He ripped the foil package with his teeth.

"Want me to do it?"

He paused to look at the vision in his bed. Flushed face. Swollen lips. Hair spread out behind her.

"Not this time." He hurriedly slid on the protection.

Staying on his knees, he grasped her hips and lifted her off the mattress. Her long limbs twined around his waist and he drove into her. She gasped, knotting the sheet in her hands.

"Did I hurt you?" he asked. Hell, he didn't want to hurt her, but her gasp had surprised him.

"No," she said, panting. "No. It's just been a while."

He withdrew. "How long?" He knew it was totally none of his business. Their pasts had nothing to do with their present. Still he couldn't stop the question.

"A year."

"But, your engagement?"

"Talk later." Her heel hammered against his butt. "Work now."

He chuckled and leaned over to kiss her. "Tell me if you don't like something. Or better yet, tell me if you do like something."

With that, he thrust back into her. He looked down to where he disappeared into her body. Her back arched, and she moaned. Her breathy moan infiltrated his very essence, driving every drop of blood not needed to sustain life to his cock. He grew impossibly, and painfully, hard.

"Faster," she rasped. "Harder."

Exactly what his mind was telling him, too. He watched his cock as it appeared and disappeared, his condom glistening from her fluids. The view was sensual as hell, and he almost lost it right then. He pumped into her, their sweaty flesh slapping together in an erotic song. A red flush appeared on her chest and moved toward her throat.

"Don't stop," she ordered, her head rolling side to side. "Harder. Don't stop."

He slammed into her, the bed rocking from the force. She cried out as an orgasm swept through her. Her channel squeezed and milked his cock as his own climax grew. His balls drew up, and he came, the forceful orgasm racking his body and leaving him shaken.

He fell against her, his breathing ragged. "Give me a minute," he gasped. "I'll move."

She tightened her legs still wrapped around him. "You feel good." Fingers threaded into his hair and massaged the back of his head. "Don't move just yet. I love your weight on me."

No matter what she said, he knew he was heavy, making it difficult for her to breathe. He kissed her ear, then left a trail of kisses down her neck and across her face until he found her mouth. Their lips sought and found each other in a gentle kiss.

"Next time will be better," he assured her.

"Not possible." She scored her fingernails down his back. "Simply not possible.

Ten

She remembered kicking away her panties. She thought they'd landed close to the door. Sweeping her foot in front of her, she searched for them. This was crazy. She could go home without them.

Her foot had already found his shirt and her pants. She'd draped his shirt over her shoulders, taking time to sniff it. It still bore the aroma of spicy cologne, testosterone, and whatever that delicious scent Eli naturally gave off. She'd decided pheromones.

A light snapped on, and she yelped.

"Where're you going?"

Turning slowly, a tad worried he'd heard her smelling his shirt, her gaze fell on an incredible muscular chest, broad shoulders, and a sleepy man. Powerful.

"Come on back to bed," he said, holding out his hand.

"No can do," she said, shifting her pants until they covered her lower half. "I've got morning chores that I have to do."

He scratched his chest, and her mouth salivated.

Lifting the covers, he scooted over. "It's warm and toasty under here."

"You're not nice," she said with a laugh.

"Hang around, and I'll make breakfast."

"Now, that's just evil." She took a step away, and her toes landed on her panties. There they were. She shook her head. "Warm bed, sexy man and breakfast? That's sort of like leading a kid into a candy store and saying, 'Help yourself.' Not fair."

He arched one sexy brow. "Who said I play fair?"

"Bad, bad man. I have to go." She bent over and picked up her panties. She heard the rustle of sheets, and before she could straighten, Eli's big hands grabbed her hips and pulled her against him.

"Bending over like that? How did you expect me to ignore that?"

She straightened and leaned her back into his chest. "Has to be a quickie."

"I can do a quickie."

She looked over her shoulder into his deep, dark eyes. "Haven't seen one yet."

An hour later, she was climbing into her car, her panties in her pants pocket and still wearing his shirt. If only she knew how to sew, she could make a pillowcase from that shirt and have that wonderful scent to lull her to sleep every night.

Who was she kidding? She'd never go to sleep with that aroma filling her room.

By the time she drove down the drive to her house, the sun was well up and had been for a while. After a quick stop to change into work clothes, she headed down to the barn, already preparing her story for when Grisham asked why she was so late.

Pedro had the entire weekend off and had gone to

Kansas to see his family. Grisham had Sundays off, so she'd expected to find him in the barn. However, his truck was missing and the doors to the barn were closed. Not like Grisham to oversleep, but anything was possible.

She moved the horses that stayed in the barn overnight out into the pasture. The last stall contained Princess and Duchess, who exited with regal tail flips and attitudes befitting their names.

Cleaning the stalls was nobody's favorite job. She tackled the work, all the while reliving last night. It had been everything, and more, than she'd dreamed. She had hoped, wished, and even dressed in her sexy undies just in case, but she hadn't really believed she'd end up in Eli's bed. The man definitely knew his way around a woman's body.

The barn phone rang, and she hurried to the office to grab it. "Flying Pig," she answered.

"Good morning, Marti."

"Eileen?"

Eileen Grisham rarely called, but her Irish lilt never failed to make Marti smile. "Aye. It's me."

"I was getting worried about Grisham. Everything okay over there?"

"Nay. The old fool fell off a ladder this morning. Broke a couple of ribs."

"Oh, no. That's horrible."

"We're at the hospital now. Don't know when he'll be back."

"I am so sorry, Eileen. Tell him everything is fine here. He just needs to get better. Pedro and I can handle things."

"Doctor's here. I've got to run."

"Keep me informed."

Poor Grisham. She'd broken a couple of ribs when

she'd been a crazy, take-a-dare teen. She'd climbed a tree and tumbled from the upper limbs. The pain with each breath had been excruciating. Basically, the only treatment had been to give the ribs time to heal. Babying the broken ribs and killing time while the breaks mended had been so maddening. She felt for Grisham. Idle time would drive him nuts.

She and Pedro would be fine. It was May, and the cattle had plenty of fresh grass shoots to eat and most of the heifers had delivered. Other than maintaining fences and checking for any late deliveries, this was their slow time, which was exactly why her parents had felt they could be away right now. If she told them about Grisham, they would certainly turn around and head home, which was the last thing she wanted. They would just have to *not* find out.

With the barn cleaned, the horses turned out, and nothing pressing that had to be done, she headed back to the house for lunch and a little rest. She'd take Rascal out later today.

A couple of hours later, the crunch of tires on gravel pulled her from a nap. She opened the door and watched Eli climb from his SUV. Her heart skipped a few beats.

"Hey," she said. "Don't tell me you were just in the neighborhood."

He chuckled. "I know I'm early, but I was done at the hospital and I saw no sense in going home for thirty minutes to kill time, so here I am."

He closed the driver's door and walked around the hood of the vehicle. Dressed in new-looking jeans, definitely new boots, and a short-sleeve Henley, he looked great, but she had no idea what he was talking about. Early?

"Um, okay."

He climbed her stairs to the porch. "You sound confused."

"That's because I am. You're early for what?"

"First, I'm late for this." He pulled her into his arms and captured her mouth in a deep, erotic kiss. Their tongues tangoed. Pretty much every bone in her body melted.

"Damn you're good at that," she said when he finally broke the kiss.

He grinned.

There was a solid tug behind her bellybutton.

"Thank you."

She gave him a crooked smile. "Is it possible you're early for more of that?"

His eyes dilated with lust. "Oh, there'll be more of that, you can be sure. But I'm early for the riding lesson you promised. Last night. Don't you remember?"

It was her turn to chuckle. "No, I don't remember that conversation." But pieces were dropping into place. Now that the memory was returning, seemed like he might have had his head between her legs at the time. "No, wait. I remember." She felt her cheeks warm. "I think I might have agreed to pretty much anything at that moment."

He smiled. "Probably. I brought a bribe."

"I thought your head between my legs last night was a bribe."

He threw back his head with laughter. "Good to know it works. But right now..." He held up the sack that'd been behind his back.

She'd noticed the white sack when he'd walked around his car.

"You didn't have to do that."

"Okay. I'll go put it back in my car." He turned and

pretended to walk away, but that wasn't going to happen. The aroma from the bag was too delicious to let leave.

"No way." She grabbed for the bag. Inside were fresh pastries from Porchia's Heavenly Delights. "Oh, man. You know exactly how to bribe me. Come on in. Want some coffee or something?" she asked over her shoulder as he followed her into the kitchen.

"Only if you're going to have a cup."

"Sit." She pointed to the table and chairs. He did, and she rounded up a couple of cups of coffee. She set the pastries on the table, got out some forks, plates, and napkins and added them to the table. "Help me eat these, please."

He took his coffee. "Had an interesting case this morning."

"Yeah? Wasn't Grisham, was it?"

He looked surprised. "No. What happened to Grisham?"

She explained about his ribs. "Sucks, but," she leaned toward him as though telling a secret, "he couldn't have chosen a better time of the year. This is one of our few slow times. Who was your patient?"

"Adam Montgomery."

"Travis and Olivia's oldest. What happened?"

"Broke his leg this morning. Was trying to get his horse to jump a fence. Poor kid landed wrong."

"Poor Adam."

"Yeah, but kids' bones heal pretty quickly. He'll be back on his horse before summer." He shook his head. "Horses and broken legs, and you wonder why I've been hesitant to learn to ride."

"Eli, riding will be a snap. Trust me."

"I do. It's just that—"

"I know. You and horses don't mix, but you will

today." She took a big bite of an almond croissant and moaned. "That woman has the magical touch."

He shoved a remaining end of a croissant into his mouth and nodded. "Uh-huh."

"Let's talk about your clothes before we go."

He looked down and then up at her with surprise. Spreading his arms, he said, "Jeans, boots, and shirt."

"Yeah but the jeans are all wrong."

"What's wrong with them?"

"They're new."

"So?"

"They're probably going to rub your inner thighs."

"Aw, shoot, Marti. I won't be on a horse long enough for that."

She laughed. "Okay, but if you'd rather I try to dig up some old jeans that might fit you, I can."

"These are fine." He sighed. "Let's just get this over with."

She kept on chuckling. "Great attitude."

"I know. I wish my mouth would sometimes let my brain lead, then I wouldn't be in this mess."

EVEN IF SOMEONE shoved bamboo shoots under his nails, he would never admit how nervous he was. Marti suspected, but she had no idea of the depth of his anxiety. He was glad they'd slept together before today's lesson. Afterward, he was pretty sure she'd look at him differently.

At the railing, Marti whistled, and a couple horses popped up. "Come on, Rascal. We've got work to do."

The dark horse—he had no idea if it was male or female—came toward them at a gallop.

Eli took a step back.

"This is my horse. Rascal is a gelding I've had for about seven years. Bikini," she yelled. A tan horse lifted its head. "That's Bikini. She's the perfect one for you."

"Bikini?"

The grin she gave him was pretty much like a solid jab to his gut. The air swooshed from his lungs, and he struggled to take a breath.

"Yeah. Bikini. Look at her markings. She's a little lighter over her flanks, like she was wearing a bikini in the sun. That's her tan line."

He snorted. "I can see it now. I'm assuming she was tanning topless?"

"Who doesn't?"

The memory of her full, sweet breasts had his cock rising to the mental vision. He cleared his throat. "Why her?" His voice was a little thick.

She patted his shoulder. "You'll love her. She's gentle and very sweet. Great for a beginner."

"I'm not exactly a beginner," he protested, a little embarrassed by her assessment of his abilities. "I've been on a horse."

"Right," she agreed. "Still, let's use Bikini. She can use the exercise."

The tan horse walked up to the railing and began to nose Marti. "She's looking for a treat," she explained. "You spoiled them with those horse peppermints."

He smiled but it was forced rather than natural. "Yeah, Bikini, remember that. I'm the guy who sent treats."

Marti led both horses out of the pasture and into separate stalls.

"Help me get the saddles."

He nodded and followed her. Shortly, his arms were laden with a blanket, reins, and a saddle.

Marti fit the bit of the reins into Bikini's mouth and fastened the reins to a tie in the stall. "Hang here," she said. "I'll get Rascal saddled, and then come back to do Bikini."

"I can put on a saddle."

"I thought you were afraid of horses."

"More like I don't trust them to not toss me off, but I know how to saddle." He knew his voice was indignant, but damn it! He didn't want her to think him a total loser. Not being able to stay on a horse was a whole lot different from saddling.

"Okay," she said. "Be sure to get her cinched tight. She'll hold her breath on you."

He waved her off. "I know all about that."

She nodded. "See you in a minute."

Jets of acid streamed into his stomach. A wave of nausea swept through him. He could do this. He'd done it before. The horse seemed nice enough. So far, she didn't seem interested in nipping him. That was a relief.

He started going through the steps as he'd learned them years ago. Plus, he'd watched Gina saddle her horse numerous times.

He could do this.

He found a brush on a shelf in the stall. Somewhere in the back of his mind, he remembered he was supposed to brush the horse's back before he put on the blanket under the saddle. He had no idea why, only that he was supposed to.

Bikini was calm as he approached her.

"Nice horse," he said. His hand shook as he touched her. She didn't move, didn't flinch. He stepped closer, the brush in his hand. Loose horse hair flew around the stall and collected in the brush. After a few strokes, he set it down, picked up the saddle pad, and put it on her back.

She remained still, seemingly not at all concerned about what he was doing.

He had no trouble setting the saddle on her back. He remembered all the little things like making sure the right stirrup and girth strap were over the saddle so they wouldn't get trapped when he hefted it onto Bikini's back. Marti's words about tightly cinching the saddle came back to him, but he was doing great. In fact, he was feeling pretty darn good about what he'd done thus far, to the point of almost being cocky. Marti would be impressed.

So he had to pump himself up to reach under Bikini to grab that strap. He winced and braced for the horse to kick him. She didn't. She remained placidly still.

"Good girl," he cooed. "Just keep standing still."

He pulled the strap through the latch and jerked it tight. After waiting for a couple of minutes for Bikini to breathe, he was able to pull the strap another notch tighter.

"How's it going?"

He whirled around and found Marti watching from the door.

"Fine."

"Remember to—"

"I got it."

"Bikini tends to hold—"

"I know. I got it."

Marti nodded. "Okay then. Let's head out. We'll take it slow." She whirled and walk down the aisle.

"Okay, Bikini. Now, be a nice horse," he whispered. After untethering her, he led her outside.

Bikini followed at a sedate pace behind him. Even though he'd wiped his damp hands on his jeans, there were still heavy sweat marks on the leather leads. His legs worked, but his knees were like jelly. He made a conscious effort to maintain his breathing, although he did feel a tad woozy.

Maybe this wasn't such a great idea after all. Maybe just saddling a horse was a great step for the first day.

He was trying to find the words to suggest that when he got his first view of Marti on a horse. With the afternoon sun behind her, she sat high in the saddle, a warrior princess prepared to battle.

"Ready?" she called from high in the air. He tilted back his head to look up at her...way, way up. His lightheadedness was taking on a headache companion. Uncertainty—not fear, he told himself—clawed at his gut.

"Eli? You okay? You're as pale as my butt in summer."

Her comment shook him out of his daze. "I'm fine," he lied. "For the first-time lesson, don't you think just being able to saddle the horse is enough?"

She studied him, and then swung down from Rascal. "You'll be fine."

"I know I will," he snapped. He fisted his hands, the leather strap biting into his palm. "I don't need to learn to ride. This is stupid. I'll be back in New York in a couple of months, and I'll never need to ride again."

Marti walked over and set a hand on his shoulder. "Eli," she said on a long-exhaled breath.

He wanted to shrug her hand off his shoulder. He wanted to throw the damn strip of leather in his hand onto the ground, get in his car, and drive away.

Looking into her eyes, he wanted to kiss her, to lose himself deep inside her.

"Eli," she said again. "Get on the horse." Her voice was a stern order.

"Excuse me?"

"Get on the horse," she repeated. "Do you need me to tell you how?"

Now, that just pissed him off. "No," he snapped again. "You do not need to tell me how." He crammed his left foot into the stirrup and pushed up until he could swing his right leg over. His behind settled heavily in the saddle seat.

Marti stood holding Bikini's halter, a little smile on her lips. "Save all that passion for later tonight." She winked and walked back to her horse. She climbed on him with a grace that spoke of years of experience.

"How long have you been riding?" he asked.

"Don't remember this of course, but Mom says Dad had me on a horse when I was six months old." She chuckled. "She was *not* happy about that. Told him if he did it again, she was going to put concrete in his favorite pair of boots. He'd explained that I would grow up around horses my entire life, and I'd better get used to them fast. Mom hadn't liked his answer, but she understood his reasoning, so that was that. I could ride alone by two years old. Of course, my horse was an old pony who probably could barely walk. Still, for a kid, I was flying on the back of a racehorse. Now, quit killing time." She clicked her tongue. "Come on, Bikini."

Upon hearing her name, Bikini took a step. Eli's heart took a leap. He latched onto the saddle horn, his hands too sweat-slickened to get a good grasp.

"Don't hold on to the horn," she said as Bikini walked up to where Rascal stood patiently. "Hold the reins like this." She demonstrated how to hold the reins between two fingers.

He relocated his hold to the reins, holding them tight between his fingers.

"Loosen up," she said. "Poor Bikini's head is pulled back."

He did as she said.

"Great. That's it. Okay, here we go."

She clicked her tongue, and Rascal took a step. Bikini followed. It wasn't too bad. His butt slid left to right with each step. At least he wasn't slamming his rear into the seat.

His thighs cramped however. Spreading them so wide wasn't a normal position for him.

"You're doing great," Marti said. "I'm going to ride ahead and open a gate. You just continue this way."

Rascal took off in a gallop, Marti moving with the horse like they were one unit.

Bikini noticed and picked up her pace. His butt bounced in the saddle, snapping his teeth together. Slap left cheek. Slap right cheek. Slap left cheek, and so it went. Reflexively, he tightened the reins.

"Slow down," he said.

But he must have done something to send a different message to Bikini. She picked up her pace to a full trot. He landed hard on his left hip. The saddle moved a little to the left. He shifted his weight to his right trying to adjust the saddle. With each hard step from Bikini, the more he felt his saddle move left. His left leg was closer to the ground now than his right.

Crap. His saddle was shifting.

Marti was riding back toward him at full speed. "Hang on, Eli. Pull on the reins to stop Bikini."

Bikini, seeing Rascal racing back, sped up, jarring Eli even more off to the left. He saw Marti's lips move so he knew she was trying to tell him something, but he couldn't understand.

Then he felt his world shift. Knew what Marti was trying to tell him.

He was a pat of soft butter on top of a stack of pancakes, slowly melting and ready to run down the side.

Marti grabbed Bikini's reins and jerked her to a stop. Eli's left leg was curled under the horse's abdomen, his ass almost totally off her back.

"Are you okay?" she asked breathlessly.

"I assume this isn't what is meant by the term sidesaddle."

She burst out into a loud laugh. "Hang on. Let me help."

A quick look confirmed that Bikini had indeed been holding her breath while Eli had saddled her. Once she started walking, she let it out, leaving the girth strap with inches of extra material.

Once Marti had the strap cinched properly and sweet-talked him into getting back on, the rest of the afternoon went without a hitch. Every once in a while, she would look at Eli and chuckle. Their ride into the pasture and back to the barn took about an hour. By then, his thighs screamed. His ass ached. His neck muscles wanted to give up and let his head roll from his body.

"You did great. Really great," Marti said as she swung down from her horse. "You'll have no trouble getting really good at this. Joe will think you lied to him." She tossed her reins over a fence rail. She looked at him. "Why are you still up there? Waiting to go longer?"

He cleared his throat and confessed, "I don't know that I can move."

She laughed, assuming he was joking. "Get down. I'll go grab some brushes so we can get these guys undressed, so to speak."

"So to speak," he repeated.

He waited for her to walk away before he pulled his right boot from the stirrup. With immense effort, he got it over Bikini's flanks, freed his left foot, and dropped to the ground. His legs wobbled and he held on to the saddle for support.

"Here ya go," Marti said, tossing a brush toward him. "Just take everything off and give her a brush down. She'll love you forever."

The brush hit the dirt with a thud. He looked at it but didn't move.

The thud made Marti turn and look at him. "Are you okay?"

"A little stiff," he admitted.

The corners of her mouth tweaked up, and he suspected she was fighting a smile. "Let me give you a hand. And don't argue with me," she added when he started to do just that. "I can unsaddle faster, and with as much ease as I brush my teeth. Scoot, and let me work." She bumped him over with her hip.

She bent over to unbuckle the girth strip, her tight little ass arched in the air. Yeah, that was nice. His argument died in his throat.

"How about I make you dinner tonight? As a thank you for today," he said.

"You don't owe me anything."

"I didn't say I did. I just thought you'd enjoy a nice dinner with some fine wine, a little conversation, and maybe throw in some stargazing."

She lifted the heavy saddle off Bikini. "Sounds wonderful. What time?"

He checked his watch for the time. Four. It would take him an hour to get home, another hour to stop and get the supplies for dinner, some time to clean up, so, he needed at least two-and-a-half hours.

"Six-thirty?"

"Can we make it seven or seven-thirty?" she asked. "I'm the only one here today, and there are a few things I need to do before then."

"Let me have that saddle," he said, and took a painful step forward.

She hesitated, and then handed it over, adding the saddle blanket to his load. "You know where it goes."

When he got back, she was brushing Bikini with long strokes. Bikini shivered, and he followed. This woman was intoxicating. The one thing he knew for sure was that he wasn't done with her yet.

Stepping up to her back, he put his arms around her waist and nuzzled her neck. "I like how you smell."

Dropping her head back on his shoulder, she laughed. "Like sweaty horses?"

"No, like Marti." He pressed his lips to the spot behind her ear. He remembered that she liked that. "Yum."

She turned her head and kissed him. "Thank you for trusting me today."

"You're easy to trust."

He kissed her, only this time, she turned in his arms to take the kiss to a deeper, hotter level. A moan came from low inside her. His gut tugged.

"If you actually want food when you get to my house, you better stop that."

She laughed. "You got peanut butter?"

"Yes."

"Jelly?"

He nodded. "And bread."

"Then I'm fine."

He chuckled and pulled her tightly against him. "Maybe I want to impress you with my cooking skills."

She leaned back until their gazes met. "Seriously? I figured you would call and get take-out somewhere."

"Ha. No way, baby. It's going to be all me tonight."

"Umm. Sounds like something I could get into."

"And you are definitely something I can get into."

She laughed softly and pushed him away. "Go. I've got work to do."

"Anything you don't eat?"

She looked at his face, let her gaze deliberately drop to his groin, and then slowly worked her way back up his body. His cock stiffened and pushed his zipper into a bend.

"No," she said and licked her lips. "Can't say that there is."

Eleven

Dinner that evening was the start of weeks of every Friday, Saturday, and Sunday together. Marti had explained that, given the time of the year, the cattle and horses could pretty much take care of themselves, so that gave her more free time than other seasons.

Thank goodness for early summer.

Their lovemaking, which had been hot at the beginning, took on an erotic, desperate need as Eli's time in Whispering Springs would be ending in less than three weeks. He wasn't sure he wanted to—or could—leave her behind. Their time together grew more precious as the clock was ticking down.

The other shadow in his life was that he hadn't heard from Midtown Orthopedics. A position there, especially a partner position, would set him up in New York and put him back inside his circle of influential acquaintances. It would be like the old days, before Gina's death. He kept in touch with doctors in NYC, and last he'd heard, they'd hired no one, but interviews had abruptly stopped in June.

When Eli had taken the Whispering Springs position, he'd assumed the New York job would be his. He'd made sure that Hank had understood that he would need to leave Texas before the end of July so he could be ready to start a new job in August. Given that his contract for Texas ended on July twentieth, he'd started putting out feelers for other potential positions in New York City about a week ago.

It was a Sunday in early July when everything changed. Like a lot of weekend mornings, the first thing he did was roll over and look at the incredible woman lying beside him. He'd gotten so used to Marti being a part of his life. Sometimes it seemed like she'd always been there.

The riding lessons, after that first disaster, had continued. Not only could he actually stay on a horse, he enjoyed their outings.

He thought back to yesterday. Joe had come out to the Flying Pig. He'd climbed from the car on two prosthetic legs. The progress he'd made in the last couple of months was nothing short of amazing. He was now talking about learning to run again.

Of course, Joe was still a teenager and had good-attitude days and bad-attitude days, but everything Eli saw was typical teen. Joe's parents' had agreed, and were in fact, thrilled with Joe's progress. They'd confided to Eli that they were beginning to see the boy Joe had been before the accident and were thankful for Eli's help.

Joe's parents had driven him out, but also along for the ride was an attractive teenage girl. She looked at Joe like he'd invented ice cream. It was obvious to anyone watching them that she was hooked on Joe, prosthetic legs or not.

Joe had clapped, whistled, and whooped when Eli

rode out of the barn on Bikini, and then took off in a gallop. Eli had whirled the horse in a circle and ridden back. At first, Joe accused Eli of lying about his fear of horses, but Marti had set him straight.

It'd been a good day.

Heck, it'd been a great couple of months. He didn't want it to be over. He had feelings for Marti, and she for him. But were those feelings enough? Or had they just been keeping each other company, knowing there was a deadline?

"Hey," Marti said, looking into his eyes. "You're awake early."

"What man wants to sleep when he has a sexy woman in his bed?"

She smiled. "You say the nicest things to me. Be right back." She hopped from the bed and closed the bathroom door behind her. In a minute, she was back with minty fresh breath.

"Good morning," she said, her sweet breath blowing across his face. "Did I remember to thank you for dinner last night?"

"Marti. You don't have to thank me."

"Oh, but I do."

She flipped the bedcovers over her head and began leaving a line of kisses down his chest to his abdomen. His cock took notice immediately and tented the sheet in race-car speed. Her tongue trailed down the narrow strip of hair that led to his promise land. He felt her warm breath a second before her lips wrapped around the crown on his dick.

He pushed the back of his head into his pillow and let out a low groan. The only way to make a blow job better was to watch. He tossed the covers on the floor, and the erotic vision before him made his heart leap into his throat. Marti's sexy body was between his legs. Her auburn hair had been pulled to the side and draped over his thigh. His dick disappeared into her mouth, and he almost came.

"Damn, Marti. You're too good at this. You're killing me."

She withdrew him from her mouth with a pop. "So you're wanting me to stop?"

The small smile on her lips and the twinkle in her eyes made him grin.

"God, no! Not if you still want blueberry pancakes for breakfast."

She licked her lips. "You taste so good, maybe better than blueberry pancakes."

Their gazes locked, she poked out her tongue and ran it along the thick vein that ran along the underside of his erection. She circled the base, then gently sucked a ball into her mouth. His breath held as his pulse pounded in his ears.

She rolled his other ball between her fingers then licked his sac, separating the two testicles. Heat flared even as a shiver ran through him. He lost his ability to think. Every drop of blood raced to his rigid cock.

After leaving a soft kiss on his ball sac, she moved back to his shaft, running the tip of her tongue around the base and up, until she once again drew him deep into her mouth.

He groaned. "Honey, I can't take much more. I'm about to come."

She sucked him deep. His cock head hit the back of her throat, and she hummed. The vibrations shook through him. His balls pulled up, ready to fire.

"Marti. Honey. I'm going to..." He groaned, fighting

the urge to release. Sweat beaded on his forehead and trickled off the side.

She withdrew, but kept her head bent over his cock. “Let go,” she said. “Let me do this for you.” Then she sank down his length.

In their time together, he’d never come in her mouth. And now, she was asking him to. His gut pulled tight. Furnace-degree heat shot through him. His heels dug into the mattress as he was overwhelmed with an orgasm so powerful, it left him breathless. Her lips clamped tight around him as she swallowed.

Afterward, she kissed the tip of his dick and laid her head on his stomach. He stroked her hair as he panted to catch his breath. Realization hit him like a kick to the gut.

He loved her.

He hadn’t been looking for this. Really didn’t think love would strike twice in his life.

He was lying there stunned with this new awareness when she climbed from the bed.

“I’m taking a shower.” She looked back with a smile. “Want to join me?”

* * *

An hour later, Marti sat in Eli’s living room sipping on her last cup of coffee for the day. It was close to eleven and she needed to get home. Grisham was back, but the broken ribs had hit him harder than she would have thought. Her parents were due back in less than a month, and she wanted to make sure everything at the ranch was exactly as it should be.

Eli’s doorbell rang.

“Can you get that?” he called from the master bathroom. “I’ll be there in a minute.”

Marti opened the door.

A tall, slender woman dressed in an expensive-looking suit gave her a quizzical look. She looked to be in her late thirties, but Marti wasn't really sure. However, she was sure that the woman reeked of money and class.

The woman's brows drew together. "I must have the wrong address. I'm looking for Dr. Eli Boone."

"No, you have the right address. Hold on. I'll get him."

Marti left the woman standing on the porch while she hurried to the master bedroom. "Eli. There's a woman at the front door looking for you."

The bathroom door opened, and he entered the room dressed. "What's she selling?"

"Oh, trust me. She's not selling anything."

"Did you get a name?"

"Nope."

He sighed and walked to the door. Instantly, his back stiffened. "Mother. What are you doing here?"

Still in the bedroom, Marti shut her eyes in embarrassment. His mother? She'd left his mother standing on the porch.

"Hello, Elias," his mother said in a smooth voice. "I didn't think you'd have company so early in the day."

"Company? Oh, you mean Marti. Where is she? Marti! Come meet my mother."

Marti finger combed her hair, straightened her shirt, and tugged at the hem of her shorts. She was not dressed to meet his mother.

She reentered the living room positive her face was flaming red. "I am so sorry, Mrs. Boone. If I'd known you were Eli's mother, I wouldn't have left you standing on the porch."

Mrs. Boone smiled. "I understand." She held out a hand. "I'm Tessa Boone."

"Sorry," Eli said. "Mother, this is Marti Jenkins, a very good friend. She has been wonderful helping me settle in. Marti, this is my mother Tessa Boone."

Marti shook her hand and said, "Nice to meet you." She looked at Eli. "I'd better run. There are things I need to get done."

"Oh, you work?" Mrs. Boone asked.

"Work?" Eli slung his arm around Marti's shoulders. "She is running the family cattle ranch while her parents are away."

"How nice," Mrs. Boone said. "An honest-to-goodness cowgirl. Don't see many of those from where we're from, right, Eli?"

He squeezed Marti's shoulders. "That's what makes her special. Now, not that I'm not thrilled to see you, Mother, but what are you doing here?"

Mrs. Boone glanced at Marti and back to Eli. "I brought you some news and I thought you might enjoy hearing it in person."

"Great. What is it?"

She looked at Marti again and said, "We can talk later. I don't want to bore your friend with business talk."

Marti might be only "an honest-to-goodness cowgirl," but she was smart enough to know when it was time to skedaddle. "No problem. I was just getting ready to leave." She stepped from under Eli's arm. "I'll talk to you later, Eli. Nice to meet you, Mrs. Boone."

As soon as she made it out the front door, she sighed with relief. Wow, talk about awkward. She rounded the corner of the house to where she'd left her car.

"Shit, shit, shit, shit," she muttered. Her purse, with her car keys, was in Eli's office. The last thing she wanted to do was walk back into that house. “Think, Marti, think.”

A figurative light bulb flashed. They’d hauled the deck chairs inside last night because of the threat of rain. Was it possible they’d left that door unlocked? She crossed her fingers and said a prayer. Then, she eased up onto the back deck and tried the handle. The door to Eli’s office opened noiselessly. She entered and was stopped short by the loud voices.

“Mother, that’s not fair.”

“Darling, you know it’s true. It’s fine to sleep with a woman like her. I mean, I do understand men’s needs. But she simply will never fit into our world. Society can be so unforgiving. You wouldn’t want to put her through that. And now that you’ve gotten the partnership offer from Midtown, you have to be thinking about your future. You need a woman who understands what it is to be the wife of a prominent physician. Can you picture her in New York City?”

“Mother,” he said with a long sigh. “Marti is a wonderful woman.”

“I’m sure she is—for a different man. Now, Dr. Vincent wants you to call him on Monday to confirm everything. I’ll be so happy to have you home where you belong.”

The backs of Marti’s eyes grew hot as tears filled her eyes. She snatched up her purse and let herself back outside. A wave of nausea swept over her, and for a second, she thought she was going to lose her breakfast. She swallowed against the tang in her mouth and raced to her car.

The urge to fly down the drive bit at her gut, but she didn’t want to confirm his mother’s impression that she was nothing but a Texas hick. She might have controlled her speed, but she couldn't control her tears. Salty drops of her soul leaked down her face and dripped off her chin.

In the time it took to get back to the Flying Pig, she'd talked herself off the ledge. She'd known going in that Eli was only here for a short time. He'd never promised her anything except good food, and on that, he'd delivered. There'd never been a discussion about the future, no plans beyond a week at a time, and she'd been fine with that.

So why did his mother's words hurt so much? Was it because she was right?

There was some reality in Mrs. Boone's comments. Marti didn't belong in New York. She'd been there. Seen some plays. Went to the museums. Had some wonderful food. But the thought of all those people crammed on that tiny island, everyone on top of one another, was not for her. She needed space. She needed open skies. And most importantly, she loved ranching. She wasn't going anywhere.

So, if all that was true, then why had she let herself fall in love with him? She knew better. She'd fought it, but her heart hadn't listen.

Eli had landed his dream position at that clinic in New York. She was thrilled for him. Sad for her but elated for him. He'd talked to her about it and about his dreams. Everything he wanted was within his reach, and she would do nothing to stand in his way.

Her feelings were hers to deal with. She'd never tell him how she felt, and he would never know. She would live through his departure. Knowing him as well as she did, he would feel awful if he thought she was in love with him and leaving would break her heart. He was a gentle soul, a caring man. She would never hurt him.

As soon as she got home, she broke their date for that

evening. He should spend time with his mother since she'd come so far to see him.

* * *

MONDAY EVENING, Marti was lying on her sofa reading a romance novel when Eli knocked on her door.

"Hey, stranger," she said. "Come on in." She forced her voice to be light and carefree. Her heart swelled at seeing him. Lust swirled in her gut. She tamped down her emotions. She knew what she had to do, and it wasn't going to be easy.

"She's gone," he announced and dropped on the couch beside her. "Finally."

"I'm glad you spent time with her."

"You should have gone out to dinner with us last night."

She smiled. "You mother came to see you."

Putting an arm around her shoulders, he pulled her closer and kissed her. "Yeah, but it would have been nice to have you there, too. I missed you."

The kiss wasn't deep and erotic. It was just a simple kiss between lovers exchanged as a hello. She would miss those. "I missed you, too."

"We need to talk."

She sat back and looked into his gorgeous brown eyes. "I know. Let me go first."

He nodded and waited.

"This..." She gestured between them. "This has been great, but I think we've run our course."

Surprise flashed in his eyes. "Excuse me?"

"You've accomplished what you came to me for. You can ride. You're over your nervousness around horses. You've come a long way. But it's also getting close to time for you to leave. I'm assuming your mother's good news has to do with Midtown?"

He grinned. "That's one of the things I came to tell you. Associate partner the first year, with full partner the second year. Unbelievable. They never do that for anyone."

She smiled, but her heart was shattering. "They're smart. They knew a good thing when they saw it." She bumped his shoulder. "You're a good thing. Wise move on their part." She cleared her throat, pushing that rock lodged there down an inch. "I know you'll do wonderful things." She hugged him, inhaled his scent, and tried to store it in her memory banks. "I'm proud of you."

"Now, my turn."

"No, I'm not done yet." She drew in a breath. "I think that we should stop seeing each other before feelings get involved."

"What?" His brow furrowed. "Why? I don't understand. Feelings? Of course I have—"

"Let me make it simple," she interrupted. "I want to stop seeing you."

"You're breaking up with me?" His voice held an incredulous tone.

She forced a chuckle. "If I had your letterman jacket, I'd be handing it over." She added a wink, trying to keep this light and get him out the door before she totally lost it. "Yeah, I think it best to end this now. No harm, no foul on either side." When he opened his mouth to speak, she cut him off. "Look, Eli. This was fun, but we're not in love. There's no reason to drag this out. I have plans for this coming weekend, and the next, you'll be packing." She stood. "I'm going to grab a glass of water. Need anything?"

He wore a stunned expression as he shook his head.

In the kitchen, she sagged against the counter. She'd never been a good liar, but she hoped, this one time, he didn't see through all the lies she'd just told. She loved him more than she'd known was possible. In all her life, she'd never felt this way about anyone, including Theodore. People survived loss every day. She'd survive this.

"I don't believe you."

She startled and looked up. "Well, believe it. I'm done. We had fun, right? Let's not fight about this. We knew there was an expiration date. I just moved it up a little."

"You said there were no feelings involved but there are. I...I care about you."

She sighed. "Oh, Eli. I care about you too, but your life isn't in Texas and mine is. Don't make this difficult."

"Will you visit me in New York?"

She shook her head. "No. We're finished. Good luck." She turned her back to him. "You know the way out."

As soon as she heard his car drive away, she released the dam holding back her tears.

Twelve

S*eptember, six weeks later*

"Have you heard from Eli?" Delene asked.

"Nope, and I don't expect to."

Friday night at Leo's was its usual crowd of cowboys, bankers, lawyers, doctors, and other singles looking for love in a small town in Texas.

Looking for love in all the wrong places, she thought.

She certainly was. Somehow the world seemed a little less colorful these days, music less melodious. Her parents were home, and everything at the ranch was back to normal.

And normal was boring.

The men in her town were boring.

Books, especially romances, couldn't hold her attention.

Television was dreadful.

There were only so many hours a day she could ride.

"I'm surprised," Tina said, pulling Marti from her mental whining. "You guys were so close."

Marti shrugged. "It was fun while it lasted. We knew

going in that we were in it for a good time, and that was all."

"What utter bullshit," Delene said. "I'm surprised your breath smells minty fresh with all the crap you're spewing."

"I have no idea what you're talking about." Marti lifted her beer.

Delene rolled her eyes. "You've always been a shitty liar, Marti. I'm still astounded Eli believed you."

"Of course he did. I told him the truth."

"Oh, so you told him that you loved him, and thought that by kicking him in the nuts, he'd leave with a clear conscious and have a wonderful life?"

"I'm not in love with him," she said forcefully.

"Yeah," Tina said. "Shitty liar." She looked at Delene. "Does she think we don't remember the last six weekends of tears and ice cream?"

"Shut up," Marti said, without any malice in her voice. She sighed. "I'm leaving." She stood.

"Where you going, Marti?" Chad asked. "The night's just getting started."

Before she could answer, Delene tugged at her shirt hem. "Don't look now, but the man you're not in love with just walked in the door."

Marti froze, afraid Delene was lying and terrified she was telling the truth.

"Hey, everyone. Hi, Marti."

Eli's deep voice rattled through her, grabbed her heart, and squeezed. Her back stiffened. Hell, everything in her stiffened. He couldn't do this to her. She was just now barely able to sleep without him infiltrating her dreams.

There was a chorus of greetings from their usual gang.

"Hi, Marti," he repeated.

She turned to look at him. Her stomach fell to her

knees, while her heart jumped into her throat. The air left her lungs. Damn it. He wore pressed khakis and a white oxford shirt with the long sleeves rolled up to mid-forearm—his very muscular, sexy forearms. His hair was a little longer, his face shaved smoother than a baby's butt, and his mouth—his full, luscious mouth—tugged at the corners with a smile.

"Hi, Eli. You're looking well." Through sheer will, she kept her voice steady.

"You, too. Mind if I join you?"

She shrugged. "Not my table. Help yourself." She turned toward Zack. "In fact, I had just accepted Zack's invitation to dance, right, Zack?"

Zack looked up in confusion. "What?"

Delene elbowed him...hard. "You and Marti were just going to dance, remember?"

"Huh?"

Delene jabbed him again.

"Oh, right. Come on, sweetcheeks." He grabbed Marti's hand and led her onto the dance floor.

"Thanks, Zack," she said, when they were away from the table.

"Sure. Don't know what's going on, but being a guy, I'm thinking I don't want to."

"It's probably better," she agreed.

Eli watched Marti and Zack dance. She wore a pair of tight jeans that showed all her assets. Her top was low and clingy, and it was all he could do not to stomp out there and jerk her away. Marti's laugh rose above the music, burning his gut with searing jealousy. His pulse pounded in his ears like a base drum. He didn't believe for one minute that Marti was over him, that she'd forgotten him.

The last six weeks had been hell. He went to sleep thinking about her. Woke up thinking about her. His dreams were filled with her laughing, sighing, and always making love with him.

His apartment was too quiet, too still. Food didn't taste as good. When he walked the streets, he thought of things he wanted, no, needed to tell her. He'd picked up the phone more times than he wanted to count. Once, he'd actually waited until she'd answered, but his voice had failed him, and he'd hung up. All his insecurities from childhood came rushing back. He wasn't good enough, smart enough, or attractive enough to keep someone like her.

A couple of times, he'd gone on dates set up by friends and family. One of the women, Ruth Smith, was the daughter of friends of his parents. His mother had been pushing Ruth on him as wife material for years. Ruth was sweet, pretty, and wanted nothing more than to be the society wife of a prominent doctor. She'd laughed at all his lame jokes, never disagreed with anything he said, and left him in the driver's seat when it came to sex. She'd let him know she wouldn't say no if the opportunity arose. It hadn't.

He'd been so bored.

He needed a woman who challenged him, drove him crazy with her mouth, and stood on her own merits. Someone who didn't give a crap about who Elias Boone was in society. Someone who didn't care that he was worth millions.

He needed Martha Gale Jenkins.

Another laugh from the dance floor had his teeth gritting. He stood and grabbed Delene's hand. "Dance with me."

She looked up with surprise, and then a smile slowly

crossed her lips. "Okay, Doctor. Let's give my friend a taste of her own medicine."

He led them onto the dance floor in time for a slow, crooning Tim McGraw song. Putting an arm around her waist, he held her and began to move.

Delene rested her hands on his shoulders and looked into his eyes. "Came back to claim your gal?"

"Maybe, or maybe I left behind some stuff I need to ship to New York."

Delene laughed. "You're as bad as she is. Both of you, a couple of liars."

Eli snorted. "That obvious, huh?"

"Eli, if this dance is supposed to make her jealous, you need to step up your game."

"What do you mean?"

Delene slid her arms from his shoulders to around his neck. "Hold me closer like I was Marti."

He pulled her in.

"Better. Now smile. You look like you're on a death dance."

He laughed, and when he did, Marti's head jerked in his direction. Her lips pressed into a firm, straight line.

"Oh, dear." Delene chuckled in his ear. "My friend does not like this."

Eli pulled her tighter. "You're a good friend."

"To both of you."

"Yes, you are. Was she as miserable as I was?"

"I don't know. Were you mopey, bitching, and impossible to live with?"

"I might've heard me referred to as a sonofabitch once or twice."

She snorted.

"I really miss her, Delene. What can I do?"

"I don't know. If you're thinking of sweet-talking her

into moving to New York City, I don't think that'll work. She hates crowds. Loves wide-open spaces. She's not made for New York. I mean, I know some people love it there. She wouldn't. You might talk her into moving, but she wouldn't be happy."

"And if she's not happy, I'm not going to be happy either."

"Exactly."

He sighed and let his mind wander. "You're saying I have to move here for her to be happy?"

"No. Not at all. But, and think about this," she said gently. "Maybe you aren't meant to be together. Maybe you had fun, even developed some feelings for each other, but in the long run, you're two ships that pass in the night."

"No." His voice was forceful. "You're wrong."

She shrugged. "Maybe so, but I don't see this working. You work in New York. She lives in Texas. Each of you are where you want to be." She kissed his cheek. "I love Marti and I want her to be happy. But New York isn't the answer. Sorry."

They made their way back to the table of friends. Marti had taken a seat between Chad and Zack, as though flanked by two bodyguards. Eli pulled back a chair for Delene and took the one next to her.

"So, how's New York?" Chad asked. "Bet you love it. All those single ladies just looking for love. What?" Chad said, and looked at Tina. "Why'd you kick me?"

She sighed and picked up her beer.

"New York is fine," Eli said. "Quite different from Whispering Springs."

"Must be nice to be closer to your mother," Marti said. "I bet you're seeing quite a bit of her these days."

He frowned. What did that mean? "Some. My parents

don't actually live in New York, but yes, living there does put me closer in distance to them."

"Wonderful." Marti's voice reeked of sarcasm.

"What are doing back in Texas?" Chad asked. "Forget something."

"Yeah. I did," Eli said. "And I came back to get it."

Marti stood. "I'm going to call it a night. Early day tomorrow. Later, gang." She whirled on her cowboy boots and rushed to the exit.

"Now what'd I do?" Chad asked.

Tina put her arm around his shoulders. "I'll explain it all later."

IT WAS difficult to find the Flying Pig ranch truck through blurry eyes, but Marti did. She climbed in, gunned the engine, and floored it out of the lot. How dare he come back and flaunt all his women in her face? Okay, so maybe he didn't do that but still... She wanted to...wanted to...

Oh, hell, she wanted to kiss him, and hold him, and tell him how much she'd missed him. She'd done a great job hiding how distressed she'd been when he'd left. Well, maybe Delene and Tina knew, but no one else had. She'd been the fun friend they'd always known.

And now here he was, totally wrecking her life again. Damn him.

She flipped on the radio, trying to lose herself in music, but then that Tim McGraw song came on, the one during which her traitorous friend had laughed and danced with Marti's guy, and she burst into tears. Damn it.

Mashing hard on the accelerator, she picked up speed, racing for the safety and security of home. Eli wouldn't be here long, probably just the weekend. She would simply outwait him. She had plenty of things to do that would keep her busy until Monday.

She turned on a backroad that was a great shortcut. There were never any cops or much traffic back here. She pushed the truck up to seventy-five, ready to be home.

Out of nowhere, a deer leapt across the road.

She slammed on the brakes. The truck fishtailed in the dirt and gravel. Jerking the wheel, she tried to compensate, tried to get the truck straight again. The deer crashed into the driver's side of the front, smashing in the headlight and hood, busting the windshield, and sending the truck careening into a ditch.

The floorboard jammed backwards and up. The steering wheel crammed down on her thighs, trapping Marti. Red-hot pain shot through her body. Blood dripped off her head into her eyes.

The excruciating agony was more than she could take. Her head grew heavy and she sagged against the door window. No one would find her until it was too late. She shut her eyes and waited to die.

"Marti. Open your eyes."

The deep male voice was exactly how she'd always thought God would sound, but right now, she was pissed at him. She didn't want to see him. He'd let her see what real love was and then took it back. Nope. She wasn't happy with God right now.

She turned her head away from the voice. "No. Go away," she said, or maybe she just thought it. Didn't matter. God would get the message.

"Marti." The same voice, but this time it sounded nicer. "Open your eyes, sweetheart."

Sweetheart? God was calling her sweetheart?

"Listen to me," the voice said. "I'm here. I love you. I can't live without you. Don't you dare leave me."

"What?" she choked out.

A hand stroked her face. "I love you. Open your eyes."

Marti forced a slit in her eyes. Bright white light hit her, and she slammed her lids shut. "No, God. I won't look at you."

The voice chuckled. "Marti, honey, it's not God. It's Eli. Look at me. Wait, I'll shade your eyes."

Someone fitted a hat on her head.

"Now, try to open your eyes."

Marti opened her lids just enough to see Eli leaning over her.

"Hey. You scared all of us." He took her hand and brought it to his mouth for a kiss. "I am so glad to see your beautiful eyes."

"Don't have beautiful eyes," she coughed out.

He smiled. "They look like diamonds to me." He held her hand tightly against his chest. "Do you know where you are?"

"Heaven?"

He laughed. "Close. Whispering Springs Hospital. Do you remember the wreck?"

She closed her eyes. Tried to remember. "I remember you dancing with Delene, and then I left." Opening her eyes, she said, "Why did you dance with my friend?" Before he could reply, she added, "You love me?"

"I love you so much it hurts."

"Why didn't you tell me?"

"I tried. You wouldn't let me."

She closed her eyes. "Sorry."

"Do you remember the accident?"

"A deer. Ran into my truck. I thought I was dead."

"Not dead. The deer lost the fight, and you were pretty banged up."

"I hurt."

"Right now you hurt?"

"No. I hurt when I left the bar. I wasn't drunk. I hadn't even had a drink yet."

"I know, darling. You don't have to talk right now."

"Throat's sore."

"Yeah. The ET tube can do that."

"Am I going to die? Is that why you're here?"

"Open your eyes and look at me." She did. "You are not dying. You broke your left leg, your shoulder and some ribs. We had to take you to surgery to set your leg and shoulder. You are very, *very* lucky."

"Did you do the surgery?"

"Doctors don't operate on family members."

"I'm not your family."

"You will be. I do love you, Marti. You've had me in a daze since the first day I met you. I want to spend the rest of my life with you. Marry me."

It was painful but she shook her head. "Can't. I love you, but I would make you miserable. Don't like New York."

"I thought a prestigious job and a fancy city would make me happy. It didn't. You make me happy. Where you are is where I will be. If it's Whispering Springs, Texas, then that's where I am. If it's McCarthy, Alaska, I'm there."

She coughed. "Alaska's too cold."

He laughed and kissed her. "I'll follow you to Mars, if that's what it takes to convince you. I love you, Martha Gale Jenkins."

"I love you, Elias...I don't know your middle name. How can I be in love with someone and not know their full name?"

"Elias Jacob."

"I love you, Elias Jacob Boone."

"Marry me? Make me the happiest man in Texas?"

* * *

November

"Ready?"

Marti looked at Delene and Tina. She'd let each of them pick out whatever dress they wanted to wear today. It honestly didn't matter to her one bit. The two dresses complimented in style and color and she'd bet Rascal they'd coordinated the purchases through Tina's dress shop. Deep purple for Delene and a deep pink for Tina. Each carried a long-stemmed white rose.

Marti stood and Tina rushed to straighten her bell-shaped gown, flipping the train of the dress out behind her.

"Your leg okay?" Tina asked. "You hurting?"

"I'm fine. Really," she added when Tina looked doubtful. "It hurts a little but the cast is off, and I'm headed down that aisle to marry Eli, even if you two have to carry me."

"You look gorgeous," Delene said. "Tina, you picked the perfect dress for Marti."

"I know," Tina said, still fussing with the skirt. "The minute I saw it, I knew it was the one. Luckily for me, she agreed."

"I didn't care what I wore. Seriously. I'd do this in the nude, if it meant marrying Eli Boone."

"Yeah, well, the guys would have loved the nude part,

but I doubt your groom would have. He's kind of the jealous type."

Marti smiled. "And so am I. I don't want you two to know just how good he looks without his scrubs on."

The three of them giggled.

There was a knock on the door a second before Marti's dad opened it. "It's time, honey."

"I'm ready, Dad. I've been ready my whole life for Eli."

Tina led the way down the aisle, followed by Delene, and finally by Marti and her dad. Eli's face broke into a wide smile the minute their gazes met.

Marti's breath caught. Lord, how she loved the look of a man in a black tux, especially this man.

She and her dad stopped at the pew where her mother sat. Marti kissed her mother's cheek and then her dad's. Her dad took a seat beside her mother. Marti didn't need her parents to give her away. She wasn't going anywhere. Eli had found his way back home to Whispering Springs and the Riverside Orthopedic clinic, joining his friend in the practice.

Eli took her hand and stared into her eyes. "I love you," he whispered.

"I love you."

They turned to face the preacher to join their lives and live happily ever after in a small town in Texas.

Photo by Tom Smarch

New York Times and USA Today Bestselling Author Cynthia D'Alba was born and raised in a small Arkansas town. After being gone for a number of years, she's thrilled to be making her home back in Arkansas living on the banks of an eight-thousand acre lake.

When she's not reading or writing or plotting, she's doorman for her spoiled border collie, cook, housekeeper and chief bottle washer for her husband and slave to a noisy, messy parrot. She loves to chat online with friends and fans.

Send snail mail to: Cynthia D'Alba PO Box 2116 Hot Springs, AR 71914

Or better yet! She would for you to take her newsletter. She promises not to spam you, not to fill your inbox with advertising, and not to sell your name and email address to anyone. Check her website for a link to her newsletter

You can find her most days at one of the following online homes:

www.cynthiadalba.com

cynthiadalba@gmailcom

Other Books by Cynthia D'Alba

Whispering Springs, Texas

Texas Two Step – The Prequel
Texas Two Step
Texas Tango
Texas Fandango
Texas Twist
Texas Hustle
Texas Bossa Nova
Texas Lullaby
Saddles and Soot
Texas Daze
A Texan's Touch
Texas Bombshell
Whispering Springs, Texas Volume One
Whispering Springs, Texas Volume Two
Whispering Springs, Texas Volume Three

Diamond Lakes, Texas

A Cowboy's Seduction
Hot SEAL, Cold Beer
Cadillac Cowboy
Texas Justice
Something's Burning

Dallas Debutantes

McCool Family Trilogy/Grizzly Bitterroot Ranch Crossover

Hot SEAL, Black Coffee
Christmas in His Arms
Snowy Montana Nights
Hot SEAL, Sweet and Spicy
Six Days and One Knight

Carmichael Family Triplets Trilogy (coming soon)

Hot Assets

Hot Ex

Hot Briefs

SEALs in Paradise

Hot SEAL, Alaskan Nights

Hot SEAL, Confirmed Bachelor

Hot SEAL, Secret Service

Hot SEAL, Labor Day

Hot SEAL, Girl Crush

Mason Security

Her Bodyguard

His Bodyguard

Mason Security Duet

Other Books

Backstage Pass

Texas Two Steps

WHISPERING SPRINGS, TEXAS BOOK 1 ©2012
CYNTHIA D'ALBA

Secrets are little time-bombs just waiting to explode.

After six years and too much self-recrimination, rancher Mitch Landry admits he was wrong. He left Olivia Montgomery. Now he'll do whatever it take to convince Olivia to give him a second chance.

Olivia Montgomery survived the break-up with the love of her life. She's rebuilt her life around her business and the son she loves more than life itself. She's not proud of the mistakes she's made—particularly the secret she's kept—but when life serves up manure, you use it to mold yourself into something better.

At a hot, muggy Dallas wedding, they reconnect, and now she's left trying to protect the secret she's held on to for all these years.

Texas Tango

WHISPERING SPRINGS,TEXAS, BOOK 2 © 2013
CYNTHIA D'ALBA

Sex in a faux marriage can make things oh so real.

Dr. Caroline Graham is happy with her nomadic lifestyle fulfilling short-term medical contracts. No emotional commitments, no disappointments. She's always the one to walk away, never the one left behind. But now her grandmother is on her deathbed, more concerned about Caroline's lack of a husband than her own demise. What's the harm in a little white lie? If a wedding will give her grandmother peace, then a wedding she shall have.

Widower Travis Montgomery devotes his days to building the ranch he and his late wife planned before he lost her to breast cancer. The last piece of acreage he needs is controlled by a lady with a pesky need of her own. Do her a favor and he can have the land. She needs a quick, temporary, faux marriage in exchange for the acreage.

It's a total win-win situation until events begin to snowball and they find, instead of playacting, they've put their hearts at risk.

Texas Fandango

WHISPERING SPRINGS, TEXAS BOOK 3 ©
2014 CYNTHIA D'ALBA

Two-weeks on the beach can deepened more than tans.

Attorney KC Montgomery has loved family friend Drake Gentry forever, but she never seemed to be on his radar. When Drake's girlfriend dumps him, leaving him with two all-expenses paid tickets to the Sand Castle Resort in the Caribbean, KC seizes the chance and makes him an offer impossible to refuse: two weeks of food, fun, sand, and sex with no strings attached.

University Professor Drake Gentry has noticed his best friend's cousin for years, but KC has always been hands-off, until today. Unable to resist, he agrees to her two-week, no-strings affair.

The vacation more than fulfills both their fantasies. The sun is hot but the sex hotter.

Texas Twist

WHISPERING SPRINGS, TEXAS BOOK 4 ©
2014 CYNTHIA D'ALBA

Real bad boys can grow up to be real good men.

Paige Ryan lost everything important in her life. She moves to Whispering Springs, Texas to be near her step-brother. But just as her life is derailed again when the last man in the world she wants to see again moves into her house.

Cash Montgomery is on the cusp of having it all. When a bad bull ride leaves him injured and angry, his only comfort is found at the bottom of a bottle. His family drags him home to Whispering Springs, Texas. With nowhere to go, he moves temporarily into an old ranch house on his brother's property surprised the place is occupied.

The best idea is to move on but sometimes taking the first step out the door is the hardest one.

Loving a bull rider is dangerous, so is falling for him a second time is crazy?

Texas Bossa Nova

WHISPERING SPRINGS, TEXAS BOOK 5 ©2014
CYNTHIA D'ALBA

A heavy snowstorm can produce a lot of heat

Magda Hobbs loves being a ranch housekeeper. The job keeps her close to her recently discovered father, foreman at the same ranch. She is immune to all the cowboy charms, except for one certain cowboy, who is wreaking havoc on her libido.

Reno Montgomery is determined to make his fledging cattle ranch a success. Dates with Magda Hobbs rocks his world and then she disappears, leaving him confused and angry. He's shocked when he learns the new live-in housekeeper is Magda Hobbs.

When a freak snowstorm cuts off the outside world, the isolation rekindles their desire. But when the weather and the roads clear, Reno has to work hard and fast to keep the woman of his dreams from hitting the road right out of his life again.

Texas Hustle

WHISPERING SPRINGS, TEXAS BOOK 6 ©2015
CYNTHIA D'ALBA

Watch out for chigger bites, love bites and secrets that bite

Born into a wealthy, Southern family, Porchia Summers builds a good life in Texas until a bad news ex-boyfriend tracks her down. Desperate for time to figure out how to handle the trouble he brings, she looks to the one man who can get her out of town for a few days.

Darren Montgomery has had his eye on the town's sexy, sweet baker for a while but she's never returns his looks until now. He's flattered but suspicious about her quick change in attention.

Sometimes, camping isn't just camping. It's survival.

Texas Lullaby

WHISPERING SPRINGS, TEXAS BOOK 7 ©2016
CYNTHIA D'ALBA

Sometimes what you think you don't want is exactly what you need.

After a long four-year engagement, Lydia Henson makes her decision. Forced to choice between having a family or marrying a man who adamantly against fathering children, she chooses the man. She can live without children. She can't live without the man she loves.

Jason Montgomery doesn't want a family, or at least that's his story and he's sticking to it. The falsehood is less emasculating than the truth.

On the eve of their wedding, Jason and Lydia's well-planned life is thrown into chaos. Everything Jason has sworn he doesn't want is within his grasp. But as he reaches for the golden ring, life delivers another twist.

Saddles and Soot

WHISPERING SPRINGS, TEXAS BOOK 8 ©2015
CYNTHIA D'ALBA

Veterinarian Georgina Greyson will only be in Whispering Springs for three months. She isn't looking for love or roots, but some fun with a hunky fireman could help pass the time.

Tanner Marshall loves being a volunteer fireman, maybe more than being a cowboy. At thirty-four, he's ready to put down some roots, including marriage, children and the white picket fence.

When Georgina accidentally sets her yard on fire during a burn ban, the volunteer fire department responds. Tanner hates carelessness with fire, but there's something about his latest firebug that he can't get out of his mind.

Can an uptight firefighter looking to settle down persuade a cute firebug to give up the road for a house and roots?

A Texan's Touch

WHISPERING SPRINGS, TX BOOK 10 (C) 2023
CYNTHIA D'ALBA

From NYT and USA Today bestselling author Cynthia D'Alba comes a steamy romance with a hot cowboy, a smart heroine and two meddling mothers who scheme the perfect meet cute.

Army Major Dax Cooper's life blew up with the IED that took his leg and most of his Delta Forces team. Medically retired, nightly dreams torture him, not only forcing him to relive the explosion time after time, but also the loss of the future he desired and is now denied. Unfocused and adrift, he follows his brother to Whispering Springs, Texas to lie low and think.

Psychologist Cora Belle Lambert understands what it's like to be an outsider. Sandwiched between two gorgeous and successful sisters, one a former Miss Texas and the other the current high school homecoming queen, and blessed with a stunningly beautiful mother, she considers herself to be the ugly duckling in her family. Determined to prove her worth, she takes on broken kids who need an avenging angel on their side. Kids. Never adults and definitely not an ex-military alpha male with sexy hard edges and mesmerizing azure-blue eyes.

Forced together on a mercy date set up by their mothers, each recognizes untapped promise in the other. Can these two broken people overcome the cruel hand of fate or will they allow their demons within to gleefully dance on their dreams?

Texas Bombshell

WHISPERINGS SPRINGS, TX BOOK 11 (C)2023
CYNTHIA D'ALBA

What happens when fate blows your life to hell?

From NYT and USA Today bestselling author Cynthia D'Alba comes a steamy romance with a hot cowboy, a smart heroine and two meddling mothers who scheme the perfect meet cute.

Sheriff Marc Singer isn't looking to remarry. Widow Dr. Jennifer Tate is focused on her career and raising her genius daughter. Thrown together sixteen years after their divorce, Marc and Jenn must face the reality that one night of passion after their divorce left them with a life-long connect. Will they find that time heals all wounds and give themselves a second chance? Can a divorced couple go home again?

If you like relatable heroes, plenty of wit and charm, and small-town backdrops, you'll adore Cynthia D'Alba's tale of beginning all over again. Tap the link to buy the book today!

Made in the USA
Middletown, DE
16 March 2025